Praise for *Dayswork*

T0191374

"Masterful."   —Alice Kelly, *Los Angeles Review of Books*

"The perfect book for a subdivided brain—a lovingly curated smorgasbord of Melville arcana lightly masquerading as a pandemic novel."
                    —Andrew Martin, *Paris Review*

"[Chris] Bachelder and [Jennifer] Habel weave a deft, subtle family drama out of one woman's obsessive immersion in the wonderful and frightening world of Herman Melville." —Andrew Schenker, *Baffler*

"Surprising and revelatory and the perfect read for all lovers of literature." —Hannah Harlow, WBUR

"What makes the novel so moving . . . is how Bachelder and Habel distill history down into a kind of personal microcosm."
                    —Nicholas Russell, *Defector*

"Bachelder and Habel have created a curious, heady cocktail of a quarantine novel that feels like a buoyant literary memoir, a surprising and exhilarating inquiry into the pleasures and pitfalls of literature, obsession, collaboration, and love, all relayed with piquant wit and thrilling insight."   —*Booklist*, starred review

"A remarkable, unusually rewarding work."
                    —*Kirkus Reviews*, starred review

"*Dayswork* is a wonder. I cannot think of another book, another reading experience, entirely like this one. It is suffused with the pleasures of reading, of immersion, of companionship in all its forms."
                    —Katie Kitamura, author of *Intimacies*

"How to describe this deeply moving and entirely original book? *Dayswork* is at once a portrait of a marriage, a meditation on art and ambition, a pandemic novel, a middle-age comedy, a brilliant collage of Herman Melville, and a tour de force of collaborative writing. Above all, it is a love story. Out of the most difficult times and unlikely materials, Chris Bachelder and Jennifer Habel have created something that can only be described as extraordinary."

—Sarah Shun-Lien Bynum, author of *Madeleine Is Sleeping*

"I was equally charmed and fascinated by *Dayswork*, this slender but capacious book about marriage and solitude, about Melville and Hawthorne, about literature and obsession and whether they might not be the same thing. Wry, intimate, and wholly original, the novel surprised me and edified me with every page I eagerly turned."

—Jess Walter, author of *Beautiful Ruins*

Dayswork

ALSO BY CHRIS BACHELDER

The Throwback Special
Abbott Awaits
U.S.!
Bear v. Shark

ALSO BY JENNIFER HABEL

The Book of Jane
Good Reason
In the Little House

DAYSWORK

{ A NOVEL }

Chris Bachelder

&

Jennifer Habel

W. W. NORTON & COMPANY
Independent Publishers Since 1923

Dayswork is a novel. Apart from the well-known actual people, historical events, and locales that figure in the narrative, characters and incidents are the products of the authors' imaginations or are used fictitiously.

Copyright © 2023 by Chris Bachelder and Jennifer Habel

All rights reserved
Printed in the United States of America
First published as a Norton paperback 2024

The authors gratefully acknowledge the following for their permission to reproduce copyrighted material: *The Atlantic* for excerpts from "And Now for a Much Deserved Moment of Insanity" by Ta-Nehisi Coates; Jerry Bryant for lyrics from "The Ballad of Harbo and Samuelsen"; Charles Olson Research Collection, Archives and Special Collections, University of Connecticut for the inscription in Olson's copy of *Moby-Dick*; Stanton B. Garner Jr. for the excerpt from a letter by Stanton Garner; HarperCollins Publishers for the translation of a haiku by Issa in *The Essential Haiku: Versions of Basho, Buson, & Issa*, edited and translated by Robert Hass; David H. Knight for his quoted recollections in *The Tower*, a documentary by Hilary Morgan; Hilary Morgan for excerpts of unpublished writing by Christiana Morgan; Rena Mosteirin for the excerpt from email correspondence; Nora Paley for Grace Paley's inscription in a personal copy of *The Collected Stories*; Sara Smollett for the excerpt from "Hawthorne and Melville, an Inquiry Log"; Thomas Travisano for the excerpt from email correspondence; Yale University Press for translations of two Issa haiku in *Field Guide* by Robert Hass.

For information about permission to reproduce selections from this book, write to Permissions, W. W. Norton & Company, Inc., 500 Fifth Avenue, New York, NY 10110

For information about special discounts for bulk purchases, please contact W. W. Norton Special Sales at specialsales@wwnorton.com or 800-233-4830

Manufacturing by Lake Book Manufacturingy
Book design by Beth Steidle
Production manager: Delaney Adams

Library of Congress Control Number: 2023016754

ISBN 978-1-324-08649-9 pbk.

W. W. Norton & Company, Inc., 500 Fifth Avenue, New York, N.Y. 10110
www.wwnorton.com

W. W. Norton & Company Ltd., 15 Carlisle Street, London W1D 3BS

1 2 3 4 5 6 7 8 9 0

For Alice and Claire,
our shipmates

Dayswork

"Bon voyage," my husband said last night as he turned out his light.

It's something he says to me, an edict inside a valediction.

"I wish you luck," he says, and said last night, I think.

Earlier he said, "Is it recycling night?"

"It is, isn't it?" he said.

"Shit," he said.

"You know how to do this," he told our younger daughter as they sat in the kitchen at what he calls the island, though it is in fact a peninsula.

(He's generally so careful with his words.)

"Combine your like terms," he said to her, I remember.

He asked our dog, rhetorically, if she was hungry.

He asked me, rhetorically, how much longer we would be disinfecting boxes of frozen waffles.

He said SCUBA is an acronym, and RADAR, too.

When I found him at a window and asked him what he was looking at, he said, "A big groundhog."

Even a quiet person says a lot in a day, almost all of which is forgotten.

Not forgotten, I suppose, but unremembered.

Some mornings I revisit a 2015 blog post titled "Words Herman Melville is Reported to have Spoken."

The list is long, and surprisingly short.

Melville said, "I do" at his wedding, reportedly.

He asked a barmaid in Liverpool, "How much?"

"Man overboard!" he shouted in 1849 on a packet ship, the *Southampton*.

This morning I see that Melville nearly missed his voyage on the *Southampton*, having waited so long to apply for his passport.

And that seven years later he nearly missed his voyage on the *Glasgow* for the same reason.

(Melville's older brother, Gansevoort, once lamented Herman's habit of procrastination, "that disinclination to perform the special duty of the hour.")

Curiously, Melville's delinquent passport applications indicate that he shrank nearly an inch and a half in seven years—
He was 5'10⅛" at age thirty but 5'8¾" at age thirty-seven.

According to ships' crew lists, he was 5'8½" at age nineteen but 5'9½" at age twenty-one.

If you had less evidence, my husband said, you'd know how tall Herman Melville was.

Or if I had more, I said.

My husband says that I seem to have contracted Melville, and it's true that some mornings we find one of my crumpled sticky notes in the sheets like a used tissue.

This blue one says, "tall and imposing," quoting Melville's granddaughter Frances.

And this green one, quoting Frances's sister, says, "Many who knew him would have said he was six feet tall, whereas he was two to three inches short of that."

While some scholars offer commonsense explanations for the discrepancies in Melville's recorded stature—errors in measurement, exaggerations in self-reporting—a medical doctor suggests that his apparent loss of height may have coincided with a loss of lumbar lordosis caused by ankylosing spondylitis, an autoimmune disease.

That doesn't sound right, my husband said.

According to a poster in his physical therapist's office, lordosis is curvature of the spine, so a loss of lordosis would have made Melville taller, not shorter.

I conceded that Melville's acquaintances noted his erect bearing.

This morning I see that John J. Ross, MD, hypothesizes that Melville's loss of lordosis was likely accompanied by compensatory hip flexion contractures, which when chronic lead to height loss.

Through my office window I see my husband reading in the backyard, and elect not to send the text I've written about Melville's hip flexion.

Dr. Ross's larger point in "The Many Ailments of Herman Melville (1819–91)" is that ankylosing spondylitis offers an "attractive unifying diagnosis" for Melville's numerous maladies, which included not only loss of lordosis, but rheumatism, sciatica, arthritis, and persistent eye pain.

[T]ender as young sparrows, Melville described his eyes at age twenty-nine.

Which Charles Olson in his book *Call Me Ishmael* misquoted, perhaps mistranscribed, as "tender as young sperms."

John J. Ross claims Melville described his eyes as "tender as pigeon's eggs," but his source provides no source.

Nor, this morning, can I find one.

[B]ut like an owl I steal abroad by twilight, Melville wrote at age thirty-one, *owing to the twilight of my eyes*.

Those eyes were small and blue and, according to Sophia Hawthorne, "quite undistinguished in any way," though she found his gaze powerful.

How he could see so keenly without keen eyes she could not comprehend.

His glance, she wrote to her mother, "does not seem to penetrate through you, but to take you into himself."

Kind of like a tractor beam, said my husband, who with his eyes attempted—unsuccessfully, I think—to take me and then the dog into himself.

Stop doing that, our daughter said.

Sophia Hawthorne's impressionistic paragraph about Melville's appearance and affect is, incidentally, "by all odds the fullest such description of Melville known to exist," according to one biographer.

Melville is "so murky," according to another, that a recently discovered photograph of a bearded man on a Staten Island pier caused excitement among Melvilleans, "even though the photo shows little more than a featureless silhouette."

According to a third, "Melville didn't want to be known; he is one who treasures, insists on anonymity."

He was born Herman *Melvill* in 1819.
And eulogized as "Hiram Melville" in the *New York Times* after his death in 1891.
And registered as "Norman Melville" on a transcribed crew list at age nineteen.

On his final sea voyage, at age sixty-eight, he was identified in a Bermuda newspaper as "A Melville."

His "lifelong smoldering restlessness," his "roving inclination."

He sailed the *Acushnet*, the *St. Lawrence*, the *Lucy Ann*, the *United States*.
The *Charles and Henry*, the *Cortes*, the *North Star*, the *Meteor*.

He climbed riggings and mountains and trees.
Pyramids, minarets, campaniles.

He Rounded Cape Horn
He Toured the Holy Land
He Deserted Ship in the South Seas and Lived Among Cannibals

Until he deserted the cannibals.

When bad weather prevented his daily walk, he paced his porch.

And Frances remembered the sound of him pacing his study—
"Sometimes I could hear him walking back and forth for a long time
and I would think how much pleasanter it would be if he were walking in the park with me."

With his son-in-law, Melville would ride the ferry "back and forth
endlessly" across the Hudson River, just for the sake of it—
"He never sat still in one seat for long, but moved about trying every
place of vantage."

Just as, years earlier, seated all day in his cold study, he sought every
vantage of the whale:
Let us now with whatever levers and steam-engines we have at hand,
cant over the sperm whale's head, so that it may lie bottom up; then,
ascending by a ladder to the summit, have a peep down the mouth; and
were it not that the body is now completely separated from it, with a
lantern we might descend into the great Kentucky Mammoth Cave of
his stomach.

And every vantage of language, history, time, civilization—

Until at an appointed hour came a knock on his door, ending his day's work.

From one of the women—his wife, mother, unmarried sisters—with whom he lived in a farmhouse in Western Massachusetts from 1850 to 1863.

From 2004 to 2011, I lived in a farmhouse in Western Massachusetts—strictly speaking, more of a Cape Cod but with a view, from the kitchen windows, of a large hayfield.

The mown paths, the business of circumference—
Hayfield, I thought to call the book I thought to write.

"It is not true," wrote Elizabeth Hardwick, "that it doesn't matter where you live, that you are in Hartford or Dallas merely yourself."

You, though, I might tell my husband some sleepless night, would somehow be in Hartford or Dallas merely yourself.

More likely I would tell him that Melville once made a list of grasses on the back flyleaf of his copy of *A History of the County of Berkshire, Massachusetts*.

> *Redtop*
> *Ribbon Grass*
> *Finger Grass*
> *Orchard Grass*
> *Hair Grass*

"He never loved any place more, not even the sea," according to the author of an article I surreptitiously ripped from a magazine at the

Subaru dealership way out on Beechmont, folding it in half, then in fourths.

September 4, 2019, according to the service records in my glove box.

In September 1850, "nearly without notice and absolutely without cash," Melville purchased his farm in Pittsfield, Massachusetts—Arrowhead, he named it.

He claimed the largest room in the crowded farmhouse for his study and, as the author of the article that I removed from the service lounge notes, installed a lock upon the door.

Or perhaps had it installed—
Many years later, when one of Melville's daughters was asked if her father was "handy about the house," she answered emphatically, "NO!"

This morning I see that Melville possessed the only key to his large study at Arrowhead.

There's a moment in Chapter V of his fourth book, *Redburn*, called "HE PURCHASES HIS SEA-WARDROBE, AND ON A DISMAL RAINY DAY PICKS UP HIS BOARD AND LODGING ALONG THE WHARVES," when the eponymous narrator hangs a towel over the knob of his locked door—
so that no one could peep through the keyhole.

In the margin of her copy of *Redburn*, Herman Melville's granddaughter Eleanor wrote that her mother told her that "H.M." occasionally used a towel for just this purpose.

Eleanor's mother, Herman Melville's younger daughter, once consented to an interview on one condition: that her father's name not be uttered.

Her father, for example, woke her at 2 a.m. to read proof of his book-length poem *Clarel*.

My husband refuses clues and will never guess the longest poem in American literature—
It's not "Song of Myself" or "Evangeline" or "That Really Long One by Hart Crane."

Clarel, the longest poem in American literature, is eighteen thousand lines of iambic tetrameter.
Longer than the *Iliad*, longer by far than *Paradise Lost*.

And Melville's daughter never forgave him.

His biographer did, however.

The most comprehensive of his numerous biographers, that is—
"legendary for his staggering precision and his devotion to his hero."

His two volumes, nearly two thousand pages.

If Melville's daughter was tired, having been awakened by her father at 2 a.m. to read proof of his epic poem, could she not, the Biographer reasoned, take a nap during the day?

And though Melville once ate a bag of oranges in front of his child, sharing none, might he not have felt himself coming down with a cold?

Or scurvy?

"This is someone who knew about scurvy from his time on ships," explained the Biographer, someone with "a need to keep his health up."

Someone with a renowned appetite.

Who, touring London in 1849, ate and drank so much he had to buy new pants.

And who, having received bad news from a publisher, wrote in his journal, *I'm floored—appetite unimpaired however—so down to the Edinburgh Castle & paid my compliments to a chop.*

Of a baked potato feast, the subject of family legend, his granddaughter wrote, "I dare not even try to remember the number I once heard were consumed by the head of the house!"

Then again, he was known to skip meals while at work in his farmhouse study.

Where he wrote facing north, at a table beneath a window, the snowy fields giving him *a sort of sea-feeling.*

Each morning he would spread out his manuscript, *take one business squint at it, & fall to with a will.*

Ishmael: *Since I have undertaken to manhandle this Leviathan, it behooves me to approve myself omnisciently exhaustive in the enterprise.*

Give me a condor's quill!
Give me Vesuvius' crater for an inkstand!

All his life, Melville wrote with quill pens, even after they were obsolete.

So concerned was he about his supply that he kept a gaggle of geese, according to one online source—
which is not, it turns out, reputable.

Gaggle or no, he fell to with a quill, "writing at frightening speed," according to Elizabeth Hardwick.

At his table beneath a window, sounding the ocean while facing a mountain:
Greylock—to whom—to which—he dedicated the novel that followed *Moby-Dick* (the disastrous *Pierre*).

Most Excellent Majesty, he called Mount Greylock.
His *own more immediate sovereign lord and king.*
The *one grand dedicatee of the earliest rays of all the Berkshire mornings.*

He climbed it, of course.

And then at the peak climbed a tall tree.
And sat on a "dangerously insecure" perch.
And shouted.

It is said that Greylock reminded him of a breaching whale.

From *A Wonder-Book for Girls and Boys* (1851): "On the hither side of Pittsfield sits Herman Melville, shaping out the gigantic conception of his 'White Whale,' while the gigantic shape of Graylock [sic] looms upon him from his study-window."

A Wonder-Book for Girls and Boys was written by Nathaniel Hawthorne—
and published a week before *Moby-Dick*.

Moby-Dick was dedicated to Nathaniel Hawthorne in ADMIRATION FOR HIS GENIUS.

Not only dedicated to, but "written at him," according to Walker Percy.
Perhaps intended to "out-Hawthorne Hawthorne."

Incidentally, *A Wonder-Book for Girls and Boys* sold almost three thousand more copies in its first two months than *Moby-Dick* sold in its first year.

And *The Scarlet Letter*, for that matter, sold in ten days as many copies as *Moby-Dick* did in three years.

(*My Dear Hawthorne:—This name of "Hawthorne" seems to be ubiquitous*, Melville once wrote in a letter that is either generous or passive-aggressive—
Well, the Hawthorne is a sweet flower; may it flourish in every hedge.)

While shaping out the gigantic conception of his white whale, Melville was deep in debt—
Including his mortgage, he owed $9,250, or over $300,000 today.

Dollars damn me, he wrote to Hawthorne.
Try to get a living by the Truth—and go to the Soup Societies, he wrote to Hawthorne.

This morning a first U.S. edition of *Moby-Dick* is advertised on biblio.com for £65,000.

(Ambitious authors deserve ghosts, Melville claimed, who would witness the adulation they begin to receive upon death—
Down goes his body & up flies his name.)

The rare edition of *Moby-Dick* is "a fine copy," "sound" and "unrestored."
The ends of its spine are lightly frayed, its corners slightly worn.
Its pages "somewhat foxed."

Foxing, I've come to learn, at age forty-nine, is browning due to age.

At age twelve, not yet foxed or frayed, Herman Melville was taken out of school because his family could no longer afford the tuition.

Months later he witnessed his bankrupt father become increasingly ill, delirious, maniacal—
"He presents the melancholly spectacle of a deranged man," wrote Melville's uncle eighteen days before Allan Melvill's death.

Soon thereafter his widow added an *e* to the family surname— though "certainly," the Biographer asserts, "for no nefarious reason"— and Herman *Melville*, age twelve, was sent to work in a bank six days a week.

The age of our younger daughter—
Presently in her room, on Zoom, in school, on mute.

On her whiteboard, beside her sister's drawing of a polar bear, she has written, "You got this!" and "Day by Day."

It's pointless, really, to imagine her walking alone through downtown Albany to her bank job, wearing a cravat.

At age eighteen Melville offered in-person instruction to thirty uncivilized students in the wilderness of Western Massachusetts—
schollars, he called them in a letter to his uncle that is both misdated

and rife with spelling errors (e.g., *systim, writting, charactars, chara-terrs, independant, gratefull, Dristict, hystory, thourough, difficultys, gen-neraly, Intimatly, Essayests, practise, delicasy*).

At age nineteen he signed on to the merchant ship *St. Lawrence* bound for Liverpool:
Norman Melville, cabin boy, 5'8½", complexion light, hair brown.

At age twenty-one he signed on to the *Acushnet* bound for the South Seas—
a whale-ship was my Yale College and my Harvard.

Herman Melville, that is, did not go to college.

At age twenty-three, having deserted ship in the Marquesas Islands, lived among cannibals, escaped onto an Australian whaler, joined the crew's mutiny, been briefly imprisoned, escaped onto another whaler, sailed the South Pacific, then quit whaling forever, Melville worked briefly as a pinsetter at a bowling alley in Honolulu.

In *Moby-Dick*, the sea, which is like everything, is like bowling, its swells *like gigantic bowls in a boundless bowling-green.*

At age twenty-five Melville wrote his first book.
In seven years he wrote seven.
The sixth of seven was *Moby-Dick*.

Moby-Dick was written "under unfavorable circumstances," according to Melville's wife, who recalled that he worked in his study all day without eating.

What Elizabeth Melville actually recorded about *Moby-Dick* is that it was written "under under unfavorable circumstances."

"Wrote White Whale or Moby Dick under"—here she turned her page—"under unfavorable circumstances."

[*sic erat scriptum*]

Thus was it written, and thus written now— under the circumstances I'm under.

Through our walls I hear the students on Zoom, mumbling their Spring Haiku.

> Sweet scent of something
> carried somewhere by something—
> Ah, something in spring.

I am so pulled hither and thither by circumstances, Melville wrote to Hawthorne in the spring of 1851, while trying to complete both *Moby-Dick* and his chores—
The calm, the coolness, the silent grass-growing mood in which a man ought always to compose,—that, I fear, can seldom be mine.

He feared, he wrote, that he would become as worn out as *an old nutmeg-grater,* and went on to complain to Hawthorne about the publishing industry: *Though I wrote the Gospels in this century, I should die in the gutter.*

Concerning the Gospels, he was correct, more or less.

Moby-Dick is "the one book that deserves to be called our American bible," according to Nathaniel Philbrick.

"[A] bible written in scrimshaw," according to David Gilbert, who, "[w]hen in doubt, or simply in need of something," opens the book at random and reads aloud, his voice "hauling forth the words like a net full of squirmy fish."

"[A]n unnatural, immaculate conception," according to Philip Hoare, who once carried around his "tiny, Oxford World Classics edition, anonymously bound in blue cloth, to be studied chapter by chapter, like the Bible or the Koran."

"I'd totally take *Moby-Dick* over the Bible," said Conor Oberst, who estimates that he's listened to the audiobook of *Moby-Dick* fifty times.

Lewis Lapham's mother read *Moby-Dick* to him when he was six.
Faulkner read it to his daughter when she was seven.
David Foster Wallace's father read it to him when he was eight.
Marilynne Robinson read it herself when she was nine.
E. L. Doctorow read half of it when he was ten—"fair sailing until the cetology stove me in."

When Stanley Kunitz was one hundred, he would ask visitors to read him a chapter of the novel—
"He looked like a little walnut sunk in a chair," said Nick Flynn, "but when you'd read he'd sort of come alive from the language."

Last night, adrift, I asked my husband to read me a chapter of *Moby-Dick*, and so he read me Chapter 59, "Squid."

. . . *the seamen rushed to the yard-arms, as in swarming-time the bees rush to the boughs.*

He turned off his light and told me that his father, a retired trumpet player, once told him that virtuosic playing makes musicians laugh— What else can you do? he said his father said.

Then he said bon voyage.

By which he meant, Good luck.
And, I'm sorry.
And, I love you.
And, Leave me the fuck alone.

Years ago—three or four beds ago—he read to me from *Death Comes for the Archbishop*, I remember, and *The Pilgrim Hawk*, and *Ethan Frome*.

He read me stories by Alistair MacLeod, Jhumpa Lahiri, Lars Gustafsson, Mavis Gallant.

He read me a story about a man who puts all his bedroom furniture on his lawn, a story about a typewriter repairman and his schizophrenic son, a story about a woman perched in a tree above a neighborhood playground, a story about a goldfish persevering inside the murk of a neglected tank, a story in which a woman who can't sleep asks her husband to make her a butter, lettuce, and salt sandwich, a story in which a boy watches a racist police officer bathe his disabled daughter, a story in which a group of boys watch a rabbi and his wife having sex, a story about a girl who raises homing pigeons in her backyard, a story about a teacher who gives Sanskrit lessons on his balcony, a story set in Peed Onk, a story set on a train to Florida, a story set at Camp Crescendo, a story in which Pooh and Piglet unwittingly dismantle Eeyore's house as they collect sticks to build a house for Eeyore—a Grand Idea that becomes, for a time, an Awful Mistake.

He read that story to my stomach, one of us having seen somewhere that this might help the baby grow accustomed to his voice.

"Gooseberries," he read to me, and "Wakefield."

Such a small bed!

Back then it was hard to stay awake until the end.

This morning I discovered a list, derived from student complaints, of the ten writers most likely to put you to sleep.

It's actually just nine writers, I discovered, because Herman Melville is mistakenly listed twice.

Over coffee, I read my husband the list of the "biggest snoozers":
William Shakespeare
Ernest Hemingway
William Faulkner
Herman Melville
James Joyce
Fyodor Dostoyevsky
Thomas Hardy
Herman Melville
John Steinbeck
Joseph Conrad

"Remember how easy it was in high school to fall asleep while reading classic novels like *Tess of the d'Urbervilles* and *Moby-Dick*?" asks the author of the article on soporific classics.

Who reads *Moby-Dick* in high school? my husband said.

Julie Taylor, I told him, is reading *Moby-Dick* in the pilot of *Friday Night Lights*.

And Rory Gilmore, I told him, is reading it in the pilot of *Gilmore Girls*.

And Heather Duke reads it in the opening scene of *Heathers*, but only because Salinger wouldn't grant permission to use *The Catcher in the Rye*.

My husband asked if any pretend boys read *Moby-Dick* in high school, and I said no.

Zac Efron does read it, I said, but he's a troubled Marine vet.

This morning I see that *Moby-Dick* has for many years been assigned to actual students at the Hackley School in Tarrytown, New York— "It's far too seldom these days that high school students get a chance to grapple with work as long and complex as *Moby-Dick*," according to one teacher of English 11.

"Yes, we read the whole thing," said his colleague.

"And then we celebrated."

One year, having completed the two-month unit on the novel, "the entire 11th grade gathered to smash Whale Pinatas in the Lindsay Room."

But I see now that in 2016 *Moby-Dick* was removed from the English curriculum of the Hackley School.

An article in the student newspaper, the *Dial*, presents the rationale for the change: teacher fatigue, student opinion, curricular diversity and variety.

"Moby Dick is a long book," according to the English Department Chair—
"It practically drives other books out of the way."

Based on what is known of the composition of *Moby-Dick*, it seems likely that Melville did not intend to write such a long book—or such a challenging one.

In June 1850, seeking an advance, he pitched the novel to his publisher as *a romance of adventure* based upon his two years of experience as a harpooner.
(He had been a harpooner for six months, if at all.)

In early August one of Melville's friends wrote in a letter, "Melville has a new book mostly done—a romantic, fanciful & literal & most enjoyable presentment of the Whale Fishery."

Melville, who then lived in Manhattan, was spending the summer at a family property in Pittsfield, Massachusetts, and in August took a break from his novel to entertain guests—
These were to be, according to one biographer, "madcap summer days filled with parties, picnics, dinners, rambles, hikes, and even a fancy-dress ball."

(Melville had invited his guests without first checking if there was sufficient room in the family home, and there wasn't.)

One morning he took a break from his break to write a review of Nathaniel Hawthorne's collection *Mosses from an Old Manse*, though he had not yet read all the stories.

By 2 p.m. he had written twenty pages.

By 2 p.m. he had written twenty pages on Hawthorne's stories, Hawthorne's darkness (*ten times black*), Hawthorne's genius, Shakespeare's genius, American genius, American critics, *the great Art of Telling the Truth*, literary ambition, originality, failure.

Pretty much everyone now agrees that he was writing about his own ambitions and resentments:
For in this world of lies, Truth is forced to fly like a scared white doe in the woodlands.
There are hardly five critics in America; and several of them are asleep.
He who has never failed somewhere, that man can not be great.

And if it be said, that continual success is a proof that a man wisely knows his powers,—it is only to be added, that, in that case, he knows them to be small.

According to the Biographer, "Melville had some food after writing all this."

As planned, he then drove one of his guests to the Housatonic Railroad depot to visit a vacationing acquaintance and the latter's new bride.

The act of writing about Hawthorne, according to the Biographer, had worked Melville into a "state of intense and undirected arousal"—
which is one way to explain why, as a lark, he abducted the young woman, whom he had just met.

He swept her into his buggy and drove away fast.

Melville always, at least until his serious accident in 1863, drove fast.

On mountain roads he was, according to one of his neighbors, "daring almost to the point of recklessness."

His family said he drove like Jehu—
2 Kings 9:20: *And the watchman told, saying, He came even unto them, and cometh not again: and the driving is like the driving of Jehu the son of Nimshi; for he driveth furiously.*

Driving like Jehu, Melville absconded with the young woman, her angry husband giving chase in an old wagon.

Back at the boardinghouse, the husband was told his wife would be released on one condition: that they attend a masquerade ball that evening.

The condition refused, someone returned the newlyweds to town, where, I see, they ate muffins and waffles before departing for Springfield.

"There is no knowing Herman Melville"—as I at some point transcribed onto this yellow sticky note—but we do know that he went to the masquerade that evening dressed as a Turk.

In a turban and robes.
With a sword, either real or pretend.
And of course his "luxuriant nut-brown beard."

Something of a connoisseur of beards, Melville was—
in fact "The Bard of the Beards," according to *GQ*.

The narrator of his novel *White-Jacket* declares beards *the token of manhood* and *the true badge of a warrior.*

In a four-chapter run he mentions beards seventy-four times.

Not including myriad synonyms:
    fly-brushes
    muzzle-lashings
    homeward-bounders

Viny locks, rebellious bristles, carroty bunches, fine tassels, nodding harvests, inflexible yellow bamboos, moss hanging from the bough of some aged oak.

Such an array of beards! exclaims the narrator, *spade-shaped, hammer-shaped, dagger-shaped, triangular, square, peaked, round, hemispherical, and forked.*
With intuitive sympathy I feel of my own brown beard while I write.

After staying up late at the costume party, Melville the Turk rose early to write.

[C]harged more and more with love and admiration of Hawthorne, he added six pages to his review by 10 a.m.—
I feel that this Hawthorne has dropped germinous seeds into my soul.

This Hawthorne was forty-six; Melville had just turned thirty-one.

Hawthorne, he wrote, *expands and deepens down, the more I contemplate him; and further, and further, shoots his strong New-England roots into me.*

After Melville's wife made a fair copy of the twenty-six-page paean, Melville added a title, "Hawthorne and His Mosses," as well as a pseudonymous attribution: *By a Virginian spending July in Vermont.*

And a geographic amendment to his botanical metaphor:
This Hawthorne *shoots his strong New-England roots into the hot soil of my Southern soul.*

This, according to one Melville biographer, is "one of the two most erotically charged passages in nineteenth-century American literature."
Lamentably, she doesn't identify the other.

(With only his iPhone and some trail mix, my husband set out from the peninsula to discover the unknown erotic passage.)

Although the reputedly Southern author of "Hawthorne and His Mosses" claims never to have met his subject—*I never saw the man*—Melville had met Hawthorne days earlier when they hiked Monument Mountain with "other local Berkshires celebrities."

Hawthorne arrived that day with his publisher in a "sumptuous" carriage—
He was, according to one Melville biographer, "the most beautiful man Melville or any of his contemporaries had seen."

"[S]o darkly gorgeous," according to the Biographer.

He was so strikingly handsome, in fact, that a woman on a snowy road in Maine once asked his walking companions, "Is he a man or an angel?"

Moreover, he dressed well, favoring a black cape and cravat.
When writing, he wore a "faded purple and gold damask-patterned robe" made by his wife.

Melville, by contrast, was "a little heterodox in the matter of clean linen," as Hawthorne once noted in his journal.

Hawthorne's son, Julian, recalled that Melville dressed such that he might be mistaken for a tramp.

He was, according to Julian, "the strangest being that ever came into our circle"—
Mr. Omoo, the family called him.

When he told his astonishing stories, he would act them out and play all the parts:
Savages, breaching whales, captains and their ragged crews.
Castaways smashing coconuts on rocks.

"The things he told of seemed to be actually taking place there in our little sitting-room," wrote Julian.
His mother once searched for "that awful club" that Mr. Omoo had brandished during one of his violent and captivating tales, but there was no club, never had been.

Melville would show up at their "little red shanty" in a shaggy coat, dusted with snow, having walked the six miles to Lenox from his Pittsfield farm.
With his enormous dog, a Newfoundland—"black as Erebus."

Perhaps in some dim attic there is a letter, foxed with age, that reveals the dog's name.

Forty miles away, Emily Dickinson also owned a Newfoundland—
Carlo, named after the pointer in her favorite novel, *Jane Eyre*.

In a letter she identified Carlo, along with Hills and the Sundown, as one of her three companions.

Her "mute confederate," she called him.
Her "Shaggy Ally."

With my three companions—my young daughter; my elderly retriever, Jacob; and Time—I used to walk past the Dickinson Homestead— On one occasion, my daughter, having learned from a children's book that dogs "can tell what people and dogs have been here even after they're gone," asked me if Jacob could smell Emily.

CALLED BACK, reads Dickinson's gravestone, past which we also walked, pausing to observe the motley offerings placed there in all seasons.

Pencils and pens, quills, coins, stones, shells, notes.

Bracelets, beer bottles, animal figurines.

"Cemeteries are more active than a lot of people think," notes the director for the tree and grounds division at Amherst's Department of Public Works.

Dickinson left elaborate instructions for her funeral, including the route by which her coffin should be carried from the Homestead to the cemetery—not out the front door and through city streets but out the back door, around her flower garden, through the barn, and across the fields.

When Carlo died in 1866, Dickinson wrote the following note to her friend:

CARLO DIED—

E. DICKINSON

WOULD YOU INSTRUCT ME NOW?

Byron also had a Newfoundland, I told my husband this morning—
His name was Boatswain.

Boatswain died at age five of rabies, I told him, but Carlo lived seventeen years.

The Methuselah of Newfies, my husband said.

Who's Methuselah of Newfies? said our younger daughter, fur-
loughed from Zoom for "Fruit Break."

The average life span of Newfies, I reported, is eight to ten years.

Didn't Byron have a bear? my husband asked.

(I see that Boatswain's brass collar, bought at auction in 2017, was
damaged from skirmishes with Byron's pet bear.)

Small things live longer than big things, my daughter said.

But hamsters, my husband said.

Why would you bring up Peanut? my daughter said.

I said that there are whales alive today that were alive when Melville
wrote *Moby-Dick*.

Not sperm whales, I amended.

But our dog could live to be twenty, our daughter said, and I agreed that as a small dog she had a longer life span than a Newfoundland.

She doesn't have an average life span, said my husband as he filled his travel mug with coffee, she just has a life span.

He then withdrew to the back porch so that none of us could overhear him teaching Intermediate Fiction Writing—
He has, in the pedagogical parlance, "gone remote."

Remote: The dark easy joke hovers unuttered.

There was a time—we've come to call it the Bad Time—when my husband went far away in our small house, the Cape Cod by the field.

(Milkweed, bee balm, prairie clover, goldenrod, Queen Anne's lace.)

I'm *right here*, he would say, wrongly.

My husband is right that I do not have an average life span, but my average life span, I see this morning, is eighty-one.

My husband's is seventy-five.

Emily Dickinson, who lived to be fifty-five, had an average life span of about forty-four.

Byron, who died at thirty-six, had an average life span of roughly forty.

As did Melville, though the numbers are skewed by infant mortality.

The next time the topic of pet mortality arises, I might tell our daughter that our small dog has an average life span of fourteen to sixteen years.

Our first dog, Jacob, who died at age twelve, had an average life span of ten to twelve years.

Our Golden Shadow, our Fretful Friend.

Dog ownership is a great way to teach children about death, according to the instructor of a class my husband and I once attended on introducing your infant to your dog.

"When our dog died," she said to the class, "I told my kids to imagine him running through a field with Jesus."

("Gracie," Dickinson once told a young neighbor while out walking her dog, "do you know that I believe that the first to come and greet me when I go to heaven will be this dear, faithful old friend Carlo?")

Our daughter, who remembers little about Jacob, remembers a shaved rectangular patch on his flank where a veterinarian tested him for allergies.

And his red plaid bed.

Julian Hawthorne remembered being permitted to ride Mr. Melville's Newfoundland when he was a boy—
At times, as he recalled years later, the dog would turn its massive head and touch his leg with its cold, wet nose.

He was also permitted to ride Melville's horse and on one occasion to sit up front in his wagon and hold the reins—

after which he said that he loved Mr. Melville as much as his father and mother and sister.

The letter that Julian wrote Melville when he was five is now "unlocated"—
[I]t is a vile habit of mine to destroy nearly all my letters, Melville once wrote.

But Julian kept Melville's reply, which was dated Monday, February 8, 1852, though February 8, 1852, was a Sunday.

I am very happy that I have a place in the heart of so fine a little fellow as you, Melville wrote.

The next day he ordered a copy of *Forest Life and Forest Trees*, perhaps as a present for the boy—
"Purchased in a muslin binding by Herman Melville for 56 cents."

Three months earlier, Julian's father had moved the family to West Newton, having tired of the "most hor-ri-ble climate" of Western Massachusetts.

"I detest it! I detest it!! I detest it!!!" Hawthorne recorded in his journal.
"I hate Berkshire with my whole soul, and would joyfully see its mountains laid flat."

While the locale had been "a paradise for the small people," according to Julian, his father "soon wearied of any particular locality."

Liverpool: "[T]he most detestable place as a residence that ever my lot was cast in."
Salem: "I detest this town so much that I hate to go into the streets."

Rome: "I wish the very site had been obliterated before I saw it."
England: "I HATE England."

The Hawthornes, I see this morning, moved at least twenty times in their twenty-two-year marriage.

On November 21, 1851, the family left Lenox in a farmer's wagon during a snowstorm, "one of the severest storms we have ever known," according to the Springfield *Republican*.

They left behind Melville—"the parched Berkshire sailor," a Hawthorne biographer calls him—and five housecats.

In his biography of his parents, Julian Hawthorne recalls that these cats chased the wagon for a quarter of a mile before settling on a ridge in a row—
"There they remained in motionless protest, outlined against the sky, until distance blotted them from sight."

The family boarded a passenger train in Pittsfield, but there is no evidence that they saw Melville before departing.

"There was nothing to be done about Melville, of course," writes the Hawthorne biographer—
"He had a family of his own."

On Google Street View I see that someone has planted a row of young arborvitae along the side yard of our former house.

The Siberian elm is gone—
"[T]he worst tree in the world," said an arborist, whose estimate for its removal was beyond our means.

The hostas we planted have spread, as have the daylilies.

By the back fence there appears to be a pet memorial stone, but I can't get close enough to read it.

An old black Lab stands outside the sliding glass doors in one of the photos on Zillow—
In another you can see its hindquarters in our old bedroom, which does not appear to have been repainted.

The partially finished basement is slightly more partially finished.

We left the rug in the makeshift basement bedroom, where some evenings my husband went to read student work and did not always come back.

I happen to know that a portion of the cement floor under that rug is unpainted because he ran out of green paint.

That's his handwriting beside some of the circuits in the breaker box.

Our older daughter's room is a home office; the nursery is a nursery.

The sandbox is a raised garden bed.

"The detached 'small' house in the backyard," according to Coldwell Banker Community Realtors, "is heated and great for an office/writing/drawing space or a child's playhouse."

"The shed," we called it.

Six-by-eight feet with a plywood floor and steep shingled roof.

One desk, one small bookcase, one lamp, a rug we found at a neighbor's curb—
One hour a day for each of us to write.

Through the sliding glass doors of the family room, the spouse with two small children could see the spouse seated in the shed, writing; through the windowpanes of the shed door, the spouse writing could see the spouse in the family room with two small children.

Time moved so quickly in one room and so slowly in the other.

I first saw the shed while driving on Route 9—
It sat in an empty field like some remote outpost, a farthest point.

A hand-painted sign provided a phone number.

I'm uncertain now, as I was then, whether $1,200 was a reasonable asking price for a wood garden shed.

We paid it, and then paid for a door, a window, a heater, an electrician, a handyman, paint, lumber, drywall, insulation, trim.

My husband dug a narrow trench for electrical wires, nailed batten strips to the siding, and painted the shed to match our house.

This morning I find in my files the building permit that my husband obtained from the town for $30—
on, I see, our fifth wedding anniversary.

The "wooden anniversary," it's called, though we didn't know that then.

That field where I first saw the wooden shed—was it really, as I remember it, a bison farm?

There was a bison farm on Route 9, I see this morning—
Long Hollow Bison Farm, no longer in operation.

Brothers Fred and Paul Ciaglo, who had grown up on the farm, bought it from their mother in 1995 for $250,000, having turned down a $1.5 million offer from Wal-Mart.

In 1998 they added a thirty-two-acre parcel so they could sustain a herd of bison—
"They dreamed of saving a small part of American history and culture by preserving the species," according to one local reporter.

"This is like our little piece of the West right here on Route 9," Fred Ciaglo said.

In 2008 they had sixty bison.

In 2013 they had forty employees to help them run the farm as well as their new bistro and market next door.

But by 2015 the business was bankrupt—
Kitchen equipment was sold piecemeal, and the land was auctioned.

"It is unclear where the bison are," a local reporter wrote weeks before the auction—
"The farm is quiet now, the restaurant closed and animals gone."

The reporter was unable to reach either of the brothers for comment.

But I don't think we ever saw any bison, my husband said.

On his computer we find pictures of our young children with goats, ducks, a donkey, a peacock, and what is either a llama or an alpaca, but there is no evidence that we took our children to see the Ciaglos' bison, their Grand Idea.

Our current selves know our former selves would almost certainly have visited Long Hollow Bison Farm, put money in the honor box, then held our children up as they took turns pouring grain from a brown paper bag into a tube that ran into the animals' trough.

It would definitely have been the hottest day of the year, said my husband.

(Cheese stick, juice box, dusty sandals.)

Some of the Ciaglo farm is now a Lowe's; the bankrupt bistro is a popular vegan restaurant owned by two Seventh-Day Adventists committed to holistic wellness and the practice of disinterested benevolence.

Pulse Cafe is temporarily closed due to the pandemic, but it looks forward to resuming its mission.

Southern Comfort Bowl, I read to my husband—
Apricot BBQ glazed tofu or soy drumsticks, cashew mac 'n cheese, braised organic collard greens, stewed black-eyed peas, marinated red cabbage.

Does that sound good or not? I asked—
by which I meant, Does that sound good or not?

I read him the burrito: marinated soy-based chicken, cheese, brown rice, black beans, pico de gallo, shredded lettuce, sour cream, and guacamole wrapped in a wheat tortilla, served w/ chips and a side salad.

That sounds good, I said, by which I meant, You would like that.

Belgian Waffle, I read, Blueberry Pancakes, Wood-Fired Garlic Knots—
by which I meant, Our kids would have liked that place.

Sweet Corn Tamales, I said, by which I once again meant, It's not so much that I hated leaving, though I did, it's that you made the decision all by yourself, in the deep vault of yourself, without me, and perhaps I would have agreed with you but we'll never really know, will we?

If he had said anything at all I would have shut up, but he said nothing, so I read to him the ingredients of the Turmeric Latte and the Acai Smoothie Bowl, and the entire list of Rishi organic loose teas.

One moonlit night in September 1850, Melville paid a surprise visit to the Hawthornes' little red cottage in Lenox.

He had news: He was to be their neighbor.

Instead of returning to his home in Manhattan, he would take up residence in Pittsfield, six miles away, where he had purchased a farmhouse and one hundred and sixty acres.

The farmhouse he regarded as temporary lodging—
He intended to build a new house in a grove on a hill with a commanding view of more than twenty miles.

His new home would have a tower—
"He is really going to build a real towered house—an actual tower," Sophia Hawthorne wrote to her sister.

("Real towered house" are among the words Herman Melville is reported to have spoken.)

Melville had already borrowed the full asking price of the Pittsfield property—
$6,500, or more than he had earned from all five of his books combined.

He had not yet put his house in New York on the market.

He did not negotiate or look at other properties.
He did not consider the necessary renovations.

(Having searched for information about Melville's wife's reaction to this domestic upheaval, I find only that she was fiscally prudent and that her "opinion could hardly have mattered.")

According to the Biographer, Melville, who previously had given no indication that he was considering a move, "was not willing to tear himself away from the vicinity where Hawthorne lived."

His impulsive purchase came just forty-one days after the now-legendary occasion of their meeting.

This morning I see that each August since 1977 the Berkshire County Historical Society has sponsored a reenactment of the famous hike and picnic on Monument Mountain—
A guide stands on a table at the base of the mountain and tells attendees, "You are about to celebrate a picnic that changed the course of American literature."

Although the 1850 hiking party drank champagne, "We stick to sparkling water these days," according to the society's curator.

I told my husband that in preparation for the 1850 hike, Oliver Wendell Holmes removed medical equipment from his black doctor's bag and filled it with chilled champagne.

The others teased him for carrying a medical bag up a mountain, but when a sudden storm caused the party to take shelter, Holmes surprised his fellow hikers with celebratory drinks.

According to one source, they passed around a single silver mug of champagne.
Another source claims there were several silver mugs.

I fear we may never know the truth, my husband said.

When the storm passed, Melville was first to the summit, having "sprinted ahead in his typical fashion."

He ventured out onto a rock that jutted forth like a bowsprit, where he hauled imaginary ropes—
to the delight of all except Holmes, who said the cliffs "affected him like ipecac."

Then a picnic in the shade with "a considerable quantity of Heidsieck."

Marilyn Monroe's favorite brand, I see—
"I go to sleep with a few drops of Chanel No. 5," she reportedly said, "and I wake up with a glass of Piper-Heidsieck champagne every morning."

There was even more champagne at the long afternoon dinner following the hikers' descent.

After that three-hour meal, the men took a riotous ramble through the Ice Glen—"another blackly romantic, Hawthorne-like landscape."

Mossy and jagged boulders, hemlocks in a glacial ravine.

The glen looked as if the devil had torn it up, according to Hawthorne, who in the icy dark was uncharacteristically buoyant.

At one point he and Melville went missing, according to one biographer, and were eventually found "deep in conversation."

I love all men who dive, Melville once wrote to a friend after attending a lecture by Emerson.
Any fish can swim near the surface, but it takes a great whale to go down stairs five miles or more.

("Sperm whales," this sticky note says, "live 'vertical lives.'")

In Hawthorne, Melville found a member of what he called the *corps of thought-divers, that have been diving & coming up again with blood-shot eyes since the world began.*

Hawthorne *expands and deepens down*, Melville wrote in his review of Hawthorne's *Mosses from an Old Manse.*
His is a *deep and noble nature.*
He possesses *a great, deep intellect, which drops down into the universe like a plummet.*

"We recognize Hawthorne's effect on Melville by the fact that, immediately upon encountering Hawthorne, Melville broke into new levels of expressive energy," according to one prominent literary critic.

At some point in the weeks after he met Hawthorne, Melville embellished his copy of *Mosses from an Old Manse*—
With sealing wax he affixed a piece of sea moss to the inside cover, and added an inscription: *This moss was gathered in Salem, and therefore I place it here for a frontispiece.*

The moss may or may not have been a gift from Hawthorne, who had moved to Lenox from Salem—
"The exact circumstances of the gathering of the moss and its travels

from Salem to Pittsfield may never be known," according to the blog of the Houghton Library.

("But then, so much about Melville is *seems to be*, *may have been*, and *perhaps*," wrote Elizabeth Hardwick.)

Even though I've been ordered by the Ohio Department of Health to stay home, I can view the pasted moss by visiting a website that digitally reproduces books from Melville's personal library.

The moss looks like flames.
But like flames underwater.
The moss looks like an aquatic bonfire, which is, I suppose, a fair representation of the state of Melville's mind at that time.

Carrying my open laptop, I searched the house for my husband to show him Melville's scrapbooking.

He wasn't at his desk with twelve tabs open.
He wasn't reading on the couch with the dog on his chest.
He wasn't mowing the lawn or filling the bird feeder or examining the splint he'd placed on the branch of a tree damaged in a windstorm.
He wasn't eating cereal at the peninsula.
He wasn't watering the plants with my grandmother's old watering can.
He wasn't jumping rope in the driveway with his new weighted rope.
He wasn't illegally streaming Premiere League soccer.
He wasn't repairing something that needed to be repaired but he also was not repairing something that did not need to be repaired.
He wasn't standing still in the garage, hands in his pockets, as though he had forgotten what he had come for.

He wasn't showering or shaving or cutting his own hair.
He wasn't walking the dog because the dog was underfoot.

He was somehow missing in quarantine—
If he'd gone somewhere, he had not left a note, or if he'd left a note, I couldn't find it.

Where are you? I texted.

And some minutes later I texted, "It is a joy to be hidden, and a disaster not to be found."

D. W. Winnicott, I texted.

I heard his phone vibrate, and then he appeared in my office doorway.

(Our floorboards, one hundred years old and nailed directly to the joists, somehow don't creak beneath him.)

Hawthorne, I told him, was known to hide behind rocks and trees to avoid people.
When visitors came to the front door, I said, they sometimes glimpsed him disappearing out the back door.

I found your gardening glove, he said.

He left before I could tell him that Hawthorne's sister said Hawthorne "kept his very existence a secret," or that his friend described him as "a fine ghost in a case of iron."

"I doubt whether I have ever really talked with half a dozen persons in my life, either men or women," Hawthorne wrote at age fifty-three.

Melville was certainly one of these persons—
They talked of "time and eternity," Hawthorne noted in his journal, "things of this world and of the next, and books, and publishers, and all possible and impossible matters."

Hawthorne appears to have liked Melville immediately—
After their meeting on Monument Mountain, he invited Melville to visit him for a few days before Melville returned to New York.

Given Hawthorne's shyness (see *Hawthorne's Shyness*, Johns Hopkins University Press, 2005), this invitation was remarkable.

Melville stayed with the Hawthornes for four nights in early September.

Sophia Hawthorne reported that Melville, who professed to be so naturally quiet as to elicit complaint, "found himself talking to Mr Hawthorne to a great extent."

According to Elizabeth Hardwick, "Melville had found in Hawthorne the lone intellectual and creative friendship of his life."

Within days after leaving the Hawthornes, Melville had borrowed the money to buy Arrowhead—
"Rationality was not, just now, the dominant force in Melville's life," concedes the Biographer.

In less than a year, he would, unbeknownst to his wife, borrow even more money: $2,050 for five years at nine percent interest.

"Don't do it, Herman!" the Biographer once exclaimed during an interview.
"Don't borrow that money, Herman!"

"But if you'd stopped him, he wouldn't be Melville," the interviewer said.
"No, he wouldn't," the Biographer said—
"But you can't love somebody and not want to warn him away from disaster."

"You love Melville," the interviewer said.
"Of course," said the Biographer, holding his hand to his chest.

"One falls in love with him," said Tony Kushner, "and I certainly have, completely, as most of the other Melville freaks have."

E.g., Hart Crane, who after reading *Moby-Dick* for the third time wrote, "How much that man makes you love him!"

E.g., Charles Olson, who after reading *Moby-Dick* wrote, "Now I burn to know, to possess the man completely."

E.g., Jay Parini, who has "sort of chased him around the world visiting spots that he visited," wanting "to somehow inhabit his soul."

E.g., Maurice Sendak, for whom "Herman Melville is a god."
Who named his German shepherd Herman.

And even, e.g., Nabokov, who disparaged Faulkner, Hemingway, Joyce, Pound, Eliot, Conrad, James, Dostoyevsky, Lawrence, Camus, Brecht, Auden, Lowell, Roth, among others.
"I still love Melville," he said at age sixty-seven.

In response to an interviewer's question about historical scenes he wishes had been filmed, Nabokov provided a brief list that included "Herman Melville at breakfast, feeding a sardine to his cat."

"Nice little morning," he added.

It's reasonable to assume there was a cat on Melville's new farm, but this morning I can find no mention of it.

I do know of a kitten in 1876.

Melville's wife, Lizzie, gave herself this kitten as a reward for having endured the composition and publication of her husband's epic poem, *Clarel*.

In the preceding months she had produced a fair copy of its almost eighteen thousand lines; accommodated her husband's obsessive revising; declined a visit from his ill sister for fear of upsetting him during proofreading, being "actually *afraid*" of the effect houseguests would have upon him; witnessed her daughter being woken in the middle of the night to read proof; tolerated the expense of paying for the publication of this poem at a time of financial uncertainty; felt "the gravest concern & anxiety" about her husband's mental condition; and mourned the death of his sister two months after refusing her visit.

A "dreadful *incubus* of a *book*," she called *Clarel* in a letter—"(I call it so because it has undermined all our happiness.)"

Debit: happiness
Credit: kitten
Balance:

(That's not quite what I'm talking about, I would have said to my husband if he were here and if we were talking about what I would have been talking about.)

This morning I see that the kitten may not have been Lizzie's gift to herself—
According to the Biographer, "someone came from downtown with a kitten in his pocket" for the Melvilles' daughter.

The cat arrived at the Melville household around the same time as *Clarel*, the production of which had taken longer and proven more expensive than anticipated.

The book, which Melville paid to publish, was in two volumes, gilt-stamped, "handsomely printed and bound"—
One hundred and fifty cantos in iambic tetrameter about pilgrims walking through the Holy Land, discussing matters of theology and human existence.

The desert they traverse is, in the words of John Updike, "transformed by innumerable nautical metaphors into a ghost ocean."

According to one reputable source, Melville wrote *Clarel* over a period of four or five years; according to another, he wrote it over a period of nearly ten years.

At any rate, he wrote it primarily during the evenings while working six days a week as a customs inspector at the Port of New York, where he earned four dollars per day.

(In nineteen years he never received a promotion or raise.)

Melville wanted *Clarel* published during the American centennial—

The poem "would be his reply to the cap-flinging and self-congratulation."

He "hoped for recognition," according to the Biographer, and "wanted to be popular again for a while."

In 1876, the year he paid G. P. Putnam's Sons to publish *Clarel*, only two copies of *Moby-Dick* were sold in the United States.

To fund the project, his dying uncle had given him $1,200—roughly Melville's annual salary.

His daughter, who was wearing hand-me-down clothing at the time, did not forgive her father for what she saw as his selfish ambition.

Take two people, my husband said last night while chopping vegetables with gratuitous precision.

Person A abandons his family, moves to Tahiti to paint, behaves reprehensibly on the island, and produces celebrated and influential works of art.

Person B abandons his family, moves to Tahiti to paint, behaves reprehensibly, and turns out to be not very good at painting.

We tend to consider Person A less culpable, my husband said, even though he made the same choices as Person B.

Moral luck, it's called, he said, as I awaited his diced peppers.

And then there's Person C, he said, who does not abandon her family to go paint in Tahiti—and not just because all international travel has been suspended due to a global pandemic—but instead works from home, makes vegetarian enchiladas, and may or may not be writing a book about Person A.

When I asked about her luck, he gestured to the air with his knife, as if to suggest I could make of it what I might.

As luck would have it, *Clarel* "landed with a thud"—
"Herman Melville's literary reputation will remain, what it has fairly become, a thing of the past," wrote one reviewer.

Years later Melville described the poem as "eminently adapted for unpopularity."

"[A]n act of defiance," Elizabeth Hardwick calls it, "a scream for the scaffold."

Three years after *Clarel*'s publication, Melville authorized, at his publisher's request, the sale of two hundred and twenty-four copies to a paper mill for pulping—
These unsold copies, from an original print run of three hundred and fifty, had been taking up valuable office space.

In 1919 an early Melvillean wrote that *Clarel* likely had a readership of one (himself)—
He was, he wrote, "presumably the only survivor."

In the first biography of Melville, published in 1921, the author doubled that estimated readership, though, he wrote, "it would be overoptimistic to presume that there will soon be a third."

According to the Biographer, *Clarel* is the best thing Melville ever wrote—

Whenever he reads the poem he begins to feel, as he reaches the fourth and final section, "edgy, vaguely dodgy and sore," because "pretty soon there won't be any more."

According to Helen Vendler, it is "one of the lasting documents of American culture."

Vendler found that upon her third reading of *Clarel* its difficulties had disappeared, and she was able to "relish the poem in itself."

Someone who posts on the Melville Society Facebook page is about to read *Clarel* for the fourteenth time—
This time as part of a book club that is reading all of Melville's writing chronologically in celebration of the two hundredth anniversary of his birth.

(One can read the Melville Society Facebook page without being a member of either the Melville Society or of Facebook, I've found.)

The book club of Melville completists has moved online due to the pandemic.

And due to the pandemic the windows in my office rattle as my daughter participates in remote P.E.

And due to the pandemic all of my library books about Melville are not due.

So many, for some reason, are navy blue.

Occasionally I find that I've brought the wrong navy blue book to bed.
As though there were a right one.

I open to some page and read until the words swim.

CLAR-el, by the way, not cla-REL, according to metrical analysis.
I've been saying it wrong in my head.

After Melville received his copies of *Clarel* in June 1876, he inscribed
just one copy, to his wife—
without whose assistance in manifold ways I hardly know how I could have
got the book (under the circumstances) into shape, and finally through the press.

This somewhat impersonal inscription to Lizzie reminds me of a story
about my husband's grandfather, a lawyer.

For years he worked an arduous and financially risky case, the con-
clusion of which happened to coincide with his wedding anniversary.
In his anniversary card to his wife he wrote:

VESTA,

THE WARNER CASE IS SETTLED.

DICK

My father-in-law told this story again when we last saw him—
In December, at the dinner celebrating his eightieth birthday.

He said his mother had saved the anniversary card and he had saved
it, too.

One day it will be yours! he told us, and all the adults laughed,
unreasonably.

Who knows, my husband said later that night in the Port Huron Holiday Inn Express in answer to my usual questions about his family.

We whispered because our daughters slept in the other queen bed.

That same grandfather, my husband told me, despised *Moby-Dick*—
He found it "prurient."

The only book he hated more was *The World According to Garp*.

You can go to sleep, I told my husband, eventually.

Too much wine, too much snow, too many hockey players in the
hall—
The morning was a distant shore.

In the dark I tried to calculate how many times Herman Melville's
heart beat:
$60 \times 60 \times 24 \times 365 \times 72.$

But 60 bpm was, I decided, too low, given tobacco and alcohol—
I won't believe in a Temperance Heaven, he once wrote to Hawthorne.

Given his appetite, his debts, his grief.
Given what the Biographer calls his "four decades of sustained misery" after the publication of *Moby-Dick*.

So I tried 75, but couldn't solve it.

Awake during winter nights in Pittsfield, Melville imagined his
farmhouse was a ship, his room a cabin—
hearing the wind, he thought he had *better go on the roof & rig in the
chimney*.
In the mornings he looked out his window as he would *out of a port-
hole of a ship in the Atlantic*.
By his hearth he kept a harpoon.

At this time, winter 1850–51, he was rewriting his *romance of adventure*, his *"Whale,"* as he then called it.

Adding cetology.
And history, biology, art criticism.
Scripture and Shakespeare.
Adding the tragic heroism of Ahab.
And omniscience.

Adding more people than he could keep track of—
forty-four named characters on a thirty-man ship, plus a "profusion of unnamed sailors."

Adding, to the dimensions he marked in his reference book on whales, "six feet to the length of the sperm whale, and nearly four to its circumference, six feet to the width of the tail."

Adding Chapter 85, "The Fountain," in which he parenthetically added the precise historical instant at which he was composing this very chapter on the whale's spout—
(fifteen and a quarter minutes past one o'clock P.M. of this sixteenth day of December, AD 1850).

[T]his blessed minute, he called it.

Melville's additions would require their own additions from posterity—
I now leave my cetological System standing thus unfinished, even as the great Cathedral of Cologne was left, with the crane still standing upon the top of the uncompleted tower.

Only small endeavors may be completed by those who begin them, says Melville (or Ishmael), and so: *God keep me from ever completing anything.*

This whole book is but a draught—nay, but the draught of a draught.
Oh, Time, Strength, Cash, and Patience!

"By purchasing a home in the wilds of western Massachusetts with the intention of supporting himself and his family on the income derived from a novel about, of all things, whaling, Melville was embarking on a quest as audacious and doomed as anything dreamed up by the captain of the *Pequod*," according to Nathaniel Philbrick, author of *Why Read* Moby-Dick?

Or, with characteristic economy, "Trees and fields and debts," writes Elizabeth Hardwick in her 161-page biography of Melville.

"[H]er booklet," the Biographer calls it in his 587-page book about writing his two-volume biography of Melville.
"[A]n embarrassment," he calls it, written by an author in "a second childhood of misplaced confidence."

The chapter in which he critiques Hardwick is subtitled "New York Intellectuals Without Information"—
The Biographer detests New York literary culture, and he loves information.

One critic, a rival biographer, once claimed that the Biographer hates an informational void and feels compelled to fill it.

"Of course!" the Biographer responded.
"I do hate voids."

He has a word for those who do not: "archivophobic"—
A word he thought he had invented until he found an earlier usage in the February 1977 issue of the *Journal of Southern History*.
("A tip of the hat to Virginia Cardwell Purdy!")

Archivophobes don't want to get their hands dirty, according to the Biographer.

As a professor he told his students, "Put out your hand."
And they never returned empty-handed—"surprised, chagrined, befouled perhaps, but never empty-handed."

The Biographer claims that in fifty years no New York publication has printed a review of a Melville biography written by a reviewer adequately acquainted with the primary scholarship—
Their Melville is "cut-down," "condensed," "truncate[d]."
An "amputated manikin."

The poor reception of his first volume by New York reviewers—e.g., "gigantic leaf-drifts of petty facts"—made it difficult for him to finish his second volume.

"Was it heroic?" he asked.

At times he sought refuge in his Bronco II, listening to a folk song about two oystermen who rowed across the Atlantic in 1896.

"The Ballad of Harbo and Samuelsen" is over eight minutes long, with sixteen four-line verses and a repeating chorus.
The songwriter, astonished that no one remembered what Harbo and Samuelsen accomplished, hoped to "provide an inspiration for folks to keep trying no matter what obstacles confront them."

In his Bronco II the Biographer "listened and blubbered."

> So all of you listening that yearn for adventure,
> Like Harbo and Samuelsen so long ago,
> Like them be prepared for the task you'll be facing:
> They were not only brave but, by God, they could row!

George Harbo, age thirty-one, and Frank Samuelsen, age twenty-six, Norwegian-born immigrants who dredged oysters at the Jersey Shore.

Seeking fame and fortune, they invested their savings in an 18' × 5' wooden rowboat, custom-built for the journey.

I showed my husband a grainy photograph of the two men rowing away from New York—
Together we stared at it like it was a Rorschach test, or like it was one of those drawings in which you can see, alternately, two different things, like a rabbit and a duck.

Like a Grand Idea and an Awful Mistake.
Like adventure and quarantine.
Like marriage, and marriage.

They packed two hundred and fifty eggs, I told him.

He nodded slowly, as if that more or less squared with his notion of the number of eggs required for a two-month transatlantic journey.

One hundred pounds of ship's biscuit, I said.

Nine pounds of coffee.

No alcohol, no tobacco, no sail.

At 5 p.m. on June 6, 1896, Harbo and Samuelsen departed from the Battery in front of an estimated crowd of two hundred or one thousand or two thousand, some of whom wept.

Samuelsen's sister, "blue-eyed Lena," clung to her older brother and begged him not to go, according to the *New York Times*.

"They are very confident that fortune is ahead of them," reported the *New York Post*, "but seafaring men say it is nothing short of suicide." The *New York Herald* commented, "Someone ought to see that this idiocy is stopped."

"We'll see you in France or in heaven!" the rowers shouted as they set off for their first destination, 3,200 miles away.

They rowed eighteen hours per day, without gloves.

They soon learned their boat would capsize if they stood, so they never stood.

Harbo logged their journey—
"Days rowing 62 miles," "Days rowing 90 miles," "Days work 65 miles," "Days work 45 miles," "Days work 135 miles," "Day's work 100 miles," "50 miles dayswork," "Drifted back about 20 mils during the day (guesswork)"

"Blowing too hard to gain any headway"
"Making slow headway"
"Making no headway"

A shark snatched Harbo's oar and followed the boat for a day and a night.
A large whale in a pod of fifty gave them "a very close call."

Their thermometer broke and they lost their anchor.
Their stove would not stay lit, so they drank cold coffee and ate raw eggs.

After forty-five days at sea, Samuelsen's watch broke—
"We feel the loose of the time very much."

(Temporal disintegration, it's called, I've learned—
The loose of the time we very much feel.)

Once, during a three-day gale, the men got no sleep.
Once, the captain of a passing German steamer shouted, "Are you
crazy?"
Once, their boat capsized and they were saved by their life belts,
which were made of reindeer hair.

"On comparing life belts made of reindeer hair with similar ones of
cork, it was found that the former was much lighter than the latter, a
very important advantage to an exhausted drowning person when he
has to put it on in the water."
(A tip of the hat to the September 1, 1887, issue of *Fur Trade Review*.)

While their clothes dried they rowed naked.
"We lost many things this time," Harbo wrote.

("[S]o many things seem filled with the intent / to be lost," according
to Elizabeth Bishop.)

Harbo and Samuelsen landed on the Scilly Islands on what would
have been Herman Melville's seventy-seventh birthday—
"*Le petit bateau! Le petit bateau!*" shouted a small French crowd.

Six days later they reached Le Havre.
With sunburn, sea boils, black-and-blue hands—
in "absolute destitution."

They could barely walk, I told my husband last night, could not shake
hands.
Both men caught a cold on their first day ashore.

Harbo and Samuelsen, I told him, hoped to get rich by making public appearances, but in Paris and London they earned little money.

In their home country of Norway, where they expected a lavish welcome, their accomplishment was overshadowed by the recent polar expedition by Fridtjof Nansen.

Nansen, I see, had intentionally locked his ship in ice, having calculated that she would drift to the North Pole.

The ship, custom-built to withstand the ice, was called the *Fram* ("Forward")—
"I demolish my bridges behind me—then there is no choice but forward," Nansen is said to have said.

The *Fram* drifted much more slowly than Nansen had calculated, and after eighteen months in the ice he set off on skis with a companion.

Before departing, he wrote a letter to his wife in case he died, or, as he put it, "if it should happen that this journey is no bridal dance."
"Remember," he told her, "no one escapes his fate."

(*Ourselves are Fate*, according to Herman Melville.)

Although Nansen and his companion were unable to reach the Pole, they attained a record farthest north latitude.

But oh god the trip back—a month on an ice floe, eight months in an ice hut, a vanished sun, a polar bear attack, a walrus attack, stopped watches, a dive into icy waters to rescue their kayaks. . . .

That they shot their dogs to feed their dogs my husband may not wish to know.

Upon Nansen's return to Norway, he was escorted by warships, greeted by thousands, honored with a celebratory arch formed by two hundred gymnasts, and invited to stay at the king's palace with his family.

There were no warships or gymnasts for Harbo and Samuelsen, though they did meet King Oscar, who gave them ten kronor— $86 today, if the online historical currency calculator is accurate, and if I've used it correctly.

They took a steamship from Copenhagen to Hoboken and, after a short stint on the vaudeville circuit, returned to dredging on the Jersey Shore.

Harbo died of pneumonia in either 1908 or 1909. Samuelsen returned to his family's farm in Norway, where he resided until his death in 1946.

Their record for rowing across the North Atlantic stood for one hundred and fourteen years.

George Harbo and Frank Samuelsen— who rowed in wool shirts and trousers, across "High sea," "Head sea," "Heavy sea."

"More sea."

The *Odyssey*: "For I say there is no other thing that is worse than the sea is / for breaking a man, even though he may be a very strong one."

In *Moby-Dick* the sea is *an everlasting terra incognita*.

Masterless and harborless.

Subtle, appalling, magnanimous, incorruptible.

Spangled and sparkling, calm and cool.

Black, bleak, mad, broad.

"You sometimes feel as you read *Moby-Dick* that these dichotomies of the ocean almost drove Melville mad," wrote Elizabeth Hardwick.

"The weight and volume of the waters had to be contained between the covers," according to Geoffrey O'Brien.

There's no fuller or heavier book, according to Ken Kesey.
Not *The Brothers Karamazov*.
Not *War and Peace*.

"[A] big kitchen sink sort of book," according to E. L. Doctorow.

An ocean, says one critic.
A voyage, says another.
A ship.
A whale—
(*my "Whale,"* Melville called it in a letter to Hawthorne).

"The real *Moby-Dick*," wrote Doctorow, "is the voracious maw of the book swallowing the English language."

In this novel, Melville "nearly touched every word once, or so it seems," wrote James Wood in a 1997 essay—
ostensibly a review of the Biographer's first volume, but in fact a vaulting assessment of Melville, metaphor, and theology.

Melville, Wood wrote, became "absolute commander" of language—
"He wrote the novel that is every novelist's dream of freedom."

Consequently, despite the decades of disappointment and despair that followed the publication of *Moby-Dick*, "one says lucky Melville, not poor Melville."

According to Wood, *Moby-Dick* "justifies Melville's life."

I place an asterisk next to the asterisk I placed in the margin of the page of the *New Republic* essay.

From my office window I can see my husband scooping seed into the bird feeders he made after his mother died and he couldn't write.

He did all the work outside, where in February he was certain to be left alone.

The feeders are copper and cedar, and they're too elegant, really, for our skinny elm and the flock of frantic sparrows.

A flutter of sparrows, it's called.
A host, a knot, a quarrel, a crew.

Each bird weighs an ounce, and yet they've worn the grass under the feeder to a patch of dirt.

What might it mean, what might it require, for a life to be justified?

James Wood was thirty-one when he took the measure of Melville, declaring that *Moby-Dick* justified its author's life.

Fridtjof Nansen was thirty-one when he intentionally locked his ship in ice off the coast of Siberia in hopes that it would drift to the North Pole.

George Harbo was thirty-one when he convinced Frank Samuelsen to undertake their transatlantic journey in a rowboat.

Paul Ciaglo was thirty-one when he bought the acreage to create a bison farm in Western Massachusetts.

Herman Melville was thirty-one when he bought Arrowhead and set out to remake his novel about whale hunting—
He was, according to the Biographer, "sure of the magnitude of the game he was pursuing all alone."

When you harpoon a whale, Ishmael tells us, *you bid adieu to circumspect life.*
[T]he swift monster drags you deeper and deeper.

But each morning before he resumed work on what D. H. Lawrence called "one of the strangest and most wonderful books in the world" and what E. L. Doctorow called "the book that swallowed European civilization whole" and what William Faulkner called "the book which I put down with the unqualified thought 'I wish I had written that'" and what Marilynne Robinson called "the most spectacular exploration of the metaphorical acts of consciousness" and what Robert Coover called the "beast we're all chasing," Melville had to give his animals their breakfast in the barn.

First his horse: *It goes to my heart to give him a cold one, but it can't be helped.*

And then his cow, for whom he *cut up a pumpkin or two.*

He lingered in the barn to watch her eat—
for it's a pleasant sight to see a cow move her jaws—she does it so mildly &
with such a sanctity.

> With such sanctity
> Melville's cow chews her pumpkin
> on a cold morning.

> It's a pleasant sight—
> the cow chews pumpkin, mildly
> and with sanctity.

> Melville feeds his cow,
> stays to watch her move her jaws—
> it's a pleasant sight.

> His day's work begins
> with a cow in a cold barn—
> so far from the sea.

> Much depends upon
> a cow chewing her pumpkin
> on a cold morning.

> He rises at eight,
> cuts a pumpkin for his cow,
> justifies his life.

After eating his own breakfast, Melville went to his study, made a fire,
then fell to with a will—
He had until 2:30.

*A*t 2½ P.M. I hear a preconcerted knock at my door, which (by request) continues till I rise & go to the door, which serves to wean me effectively from my writing, however interested I may be.

Perhaps "effectually," not "effectively," given Melville's wretched handwriting.

The person knocking was one of the numerous women in the house—his wife, mother, three sisters.
Or one of the two Irish servants, both named Mary.

One of Melville's friends called him a "Blue-Beard who has hidden away five agreeable ladies in an icy glen."

He was, according to the Biographer, "a family man, indulged, even pampered."
Another biographer claims that the "women of the house treated Melville like a pasha."

"The Author," his sister Augusta called him in her record of family outings—
e.g., "vehicle—carriage—party—The Author, his mother, & wife & sister Augusta."

Augusta was "Herman's most understanding sister," according to his granddaughter, and also his favorite—

Gus, he called her.

"Who are you writing to Gus?" Melville is reported to have spoken—
"Well, give her my very best love."

Augusta was a "supreme" correspondent, who for years kept a
record—in two notebooks, sewn together—of every letter she sent
and received.

Her letter-writing, however, was frequently interrupted by her brother's daily need of a copyist—
"Herman came in with another batch of copying which he was most
anxious to have as soon as possible," she once wrote.

One scholar called her "exhaustless in copying manuscript," although
at least one of her letters shows her to be exhausted—
"My hand is so weary of holding a pen, the fingers relaxed their grasp
upon it, without my will."

Augusta was the primary copyist of *Moby-Dick* and consequently its
first reader.
"That book of his will create a great interest I think," she wrote in
May 1851—
"It is very fine."

With the exception of *Billy Budd*, found in Melville's desk after his
death, all of his prose was copied by the women in his family.

As they produced clean copies of his manuscripts they omitted punctuation, at Melville's request, so that he could add it—
"This practice, incidentally, was not altogether a fortunate one,"
according to the author of the dissertation "Melville's Wife: A Study
of Elizabeth Shaw Melville."

It was not fortunate for the manuscript because Melville, in his impatience, often neglected to add punctuation.

And not fortunate for Elizabeth because of its effect upon her own writing.

In a letter to her mother she explained, "if there is no punctuation marks you must make them yourself for when I copy I do not punctuate at all but leave it for a final revision for Herman."
"I have got so used to write without I cannot always think of it."

She had been a precocious child, unlike Melville, whose father called him at age seven "very backward in speech & somewhat slow in comprehension."

Whereas Melville was forced to leave school at age twelve, Elizabeth attended prominent private schools until she was almost nineteen. According to one biographer, "her punctuation (her spelling, too, for that matter) was far superior to that of anyone in the Melville family, including Herman."

(Who once called "daguerreotype" *a devel of an unspellable word*.)

In another letter to her mother Elizabeth wrote, "I cannot write any more—it makes me terribly nervous—I don't know as you can read this I have scribbled it so, but I can't help it—do excuse and burn it."

The omission of punctuation was just one of the challenges Melville's wife faced when copying his manuscripts—
e.g., his "cross-outs, revisions, carets, circles," his "chaotic obliteration of the page," his "cabalistic hand."

"When the demons directed him, Melville's hand deteriorated"—

One prominent critic wrote of a Melville manuscript that the "text before me soon became an object that defied perception."

In the case of such illegibility, he argues, transcription becomes interpretation—
Inevitably, transcribers' choices evince their "rhetorical agendas."

One "scribble" that he deciphers as *promotion*, the Biographer reads as *peroration*.

"The word I transcribe as 'peroration' is NOT an illegible word," writes the Biographer, who for years woke in the middle of the night to devote extra hours to deciphering Melville's handwriting.

"It is what Melville intended it to be," he claims on his blog.

"Are we in a textual kindergarten where we make every child feel equally proud of himself or herself?" he asks.
"What Jimmy transcribes is just as good as what Suzie transcribes?"

He began his blog in 2011 to rebut falsehoods, correct errors, and defend his scholarship—
to "lay out the truth."

Five thousand five hundred and two posts and seventy-three follow-ers as of today, whatever day it is.

Today—*this blessed minute*—the hawk is back, perched on the roof of our neighbor's dilapidated shed.

Consequently, our small dog is not permitted to go out in the yard, and waits uncomprehendingly by the back door.

Maybe later, my husband tells her.

He's heard that dog tags have been found in the nests of hawks—
Or maybe it was the nests of eagles, he said.

"Fact check: Could a hawk actually fly away with your tiny dog?"
No, according to the freelance nature writer, who does not recommend attaching small weights to your dog.

"That's a creative idea," she writes, "but probably not necessary."

Red-tailed hawks weigh about three pounds and cannot carry more than their body weight, so our eight-pound dog is not in danger.

But still we don't let her out.

For in this world of lies, Truth is forced to fly like a scared white doe in the woodlands.

Or perhaps a *sacred* white doe.

When copying "Hawthorne and His Mosses," Melville's wife wrote "scared."
Which the Biographer, quoting the passage in his biography, amended to "sacred."

"In Melville, Truth is apt to be holy, even if secretive," he reasoned, and therefore the word "scared" is "plausible but less fraught with Melvillean meanings."

He admits to having made this alteration—that is, to having corrected Melville's wife—"edgily."

The nearly illegible manuscripts of male geniuses:
One of Victor Hugo's publishers likened his writing to a "battlefield on a piece of paper."
One of Balzac's manuscripts allegedly drove a typesetter to insanity.
As for Robert Louis Stevenson, "No printer ever could make out what he had written."

"Your Lordships MS. was very difficult to decypher," Mary Shelley wrote to Lord Byron, "so pardon blunders & omissions."
As his primary copyist, she became accustomed to his "letterless scrawl."

Sophia Tolstoy stayed up late with a candle and a magnifying glass and the day's pages of *War and Peace*.

She copied *War and Peace* seven times, I told my husband while he read online reviews of propane heaters.

That's a lot, he said.

We're well past the point in our marriage when we might fight about the Tolstoys' division of labor.

"What a labor of Hercules it was, to decipher this sorcerer's spellbook covered with lines furiously scratched out, corrections colliding with each other, sibylline balloons floating in the margins, prickly afterthoughts sprawled all over the page."

"Often the author himself could not make out what he had written."

According to one of Tolstoy's biographers, Sophia's work on her husband's manuscripts constituted her "greatest source of pleasure."

"This is the way for gifted, energetic wives of writers to a sort of composition of their own," according to Elizabeth Hardwick—
A "peculiar illusion of collaboration," she called it in one of her essays collected in *Seduction and Betrayal*.

These essays were written after her husband, Robert Lowell, left her for Lady Caroline Blackwood, an English writer and heir to the Guinness fortune.

Lowell and Hardwick were both fifty-three at the time; their daughter, Harriet, was in the seventh grade.

Ultimately, their separation led to an intensely productive period for Hardwick, who was, according to Harriet, "never freer or more lively" than in those years—
She experienced, her friend Mary McCarthy noted, a "certain euphoria (60%) about living alone."

But initially she sent long letters to Lowell in England, pleading for his return—
for the sake of their daughter, for the sake of his health and dignity, and for the sake of American literature.

"You are a great American writer," she wrote to him—
"You have told us what we are, like Melville."

Lowell's letters to Hardwick at this time chart his ambivalence:
October 18, 1970, to "Dearest Lizzie": "I don't think I can come back to you."
November 7, 1970, to "Dearest Lizzie": "Maybe you could take me back."
November 30, 1970, to "Dearest Lizzie": "I still do nothing much but bury my indecisions in many many poems."

"My Dearest Lizzie," I see this morning, is the salutation of the only surviving letter from Melville to his wife, Elizabeth Shaw Melville. (The others appear to have been destroyed by their younger daughter, the one who objected to hearing his name.)

This sole surviving letter was written in March 1861 from Washington, D.C., where he was seeking (unsuccessfully, it turned out) a consulship in Florence—
one of the sort that Hawthorne, who was "in every way a more plausible man and citizen than Melville," according to Elizabeth Hardwick, had held in Liverpool from 1853 to 1857.

While in Washington, Melville attended a reception at the White House and waited in line to meet President Lincoln—
Old Able [sic] *is much better looking that* [sic] *I expected & younger looking*, he wrote to Lizzie.
He shook hands like a good fellow—working hard at it like a man sawing wood at so much per cord.

Mrs. Lincoln he found *rather good-looking* and the furniture *[s]upurb.*

[sic semper tyrannis]

The next morning he added a brief postscript reporting that he felt *rather overdone.*

Kisses to the children, he wrote.

Hope to get a letter from you today
                    Thine, My Dearest Lizzie
                                Herman

They had been married almost fourteen years and had four children.

Their marriage, according to Hardwick, "was more prudent for Melville than for his wife."

Elizabeth Shaw was the daughter of Lemuel Shaw, chief justice of the Supreme Judicial Court of Massachusetts from 1830 to 1860—
A United States Supreme Court justice called Shaw "the greatest magistrate which this country has produced."

The Shaw family resided on Beacon Hill in a large home on Mount Vernon Street—
Roughly five blocks, I see on Google Maps, from Robert Lowell's childhood home.

Lizzie Shaw was "as guileless as she was wealthy," "good-natured," "friendly," "steady," "very happy and very, very good."

Melville was a handsome adventurer, genteel but rough-hewn, the author of sensational and salacious tales from the South Seas.

The recipient of fan mail from swooning women—
e.g., "you dear creature, I want to see you so amazingly."

Melville was, according to the Biographer, nothing less than "the first American literary sex symbol."

When Emily Dickinson's father caught her reading *Typee*, he "advised wiser employment" and later at family devotions read from Matthew the parable about the man with one talent—
"I think he thought my conscience would adjust the gender," Dickinson explained.

Although *Typee* and *Omoo*, Melville's first two books, constituted what Hardwick calls "property of a kind," Melville could not support himself, let alone a wife.

The swashbuckling sex symbol lived with his mother.

Melville's domineering mother was said to have "used a steering oar" to effectuate her son's financially advantageous alliance with the Shaws.

Judge Shaw had a warm and long-standing relationship with the Melvilles, but if he'd known how little Melville earned from his first two books, he would have had "good reason to worry about his daughter's future."

The groom was twenty-eight and the bride twenty-five when they married on August 4, 1847, at the Shaw residence in a ceremony "attended by troops of Beacon Hill worthies."

Lizzie preferred a church but feared that if news of the wedding spread, "a great crowd might rush out of mere curiosity to see 'the author.'"

On the morning of the wedding Melville took a walk on the Common.
Or, "Herman sallied out early in the forenoon for his last vagabondizing as an unmarried man," in the words of the Biographer.

Whose blog entry for today, I see, reports a frustrating transaction with Netflix:
He ordered the BBC's *Cymbeline* starring Helen Mirren, but instead received a "hyper-violent" version from 2015 featuring dirty cops and a biker gang.

"Sealed it up and sent it back."

Which must mean, my husband pointed out, that the Biographer still has a DVD subscription to Netflix.

Not wanting to pay to access the movie through Amazon Prime, he ordered a copy on eBay, asking the seller to make sure it wasn't the violent biker version.

For days, according to his blog, the Biographer has been yearning to listen to the Act V recognition scene in the BBC version of *Cymbeline*.

Earlier this year he wrote that while doing exercises in the middle of the night he'd been listening to film adaptations of Shakespeare, including some other version of *Cymbeline*—
"Nothing more consoling than Act 5 over and over."

In 1956, at age twenty, while recovering from tuberculosis, he did nothing but read and reread all the plays in his one-volume Shakespeare—
in an 8' × 9' room that he calls "sacred."

His careful notes in the volume indicate that he read *Hamlet* ten times, *Othello* eleven times, *The Tempest* sixteen times, *Measure for Measure* seventeen times.

He remembers these five months of bed rest as a great adventure.

Like the Biographer, Melville had a recumbent conversion to Shakespeare—
on a sofa in his in-laws' house on Beacon Hill, while his wife recovered from the birth of their first child.

Dolt & ass that I am, he wrote to a friend, *I have lived more than 29 years, & until a few days ago, never made close acquaintance with the divine William.*

He had finally found an edition of Shakespeare with a font size he found legible—
glorious great type, every letter whereof is a soldier, & the top of every "t" like a musket barrel.

His eyes, *tender as young sparrows,* could not endure small print—
They may have been weakened, I've just learned, by scarlet fever, which, I've somehow just learned, he contracted as a boy.

Having found this large-print edition of Shakespeare, Melville passed most of his time at his in-laws' lounging on a sofa and reading.

After his months with Shakespeare, the Biographer, still convalescing in the afternoons, read *Moby-Dick* over the course of eleven days—
"I was astounded that an American writer had absorbed Shakespeare so profoundly."

One journalist who interviewed the Biographer suggests that he began to identify with Melville, who like him was an autodidact and an obsessive reader.

And who like him had lost an older brother.

The Biographer's brother, Wilburn, was electrocuted while unloading metal pipes.
Three other workers survived, but Wilburn had nails poking through the thin soles of his old shoes—
"The nails did it," the Biographer wrote on his blog.

"You want to know what his death did to the family," the Biographer wrote of his brother, "read about Gansevoort Melville's death in the first volume of my biography."

Talking to a journalist about his brother forty years after his death, the Biographer began to sob.

> The weariest and most loathed worldly life
> That age, ache, penury and imprisonment
> Can lay on nature is a paradise
> To what we fear of death.

Melville's ailing brother, Gansevoort, copied these lines from *Measure for Measure* and included them, or may have included them, in a letter sent to Herman from London, April 3, 1846.

Gansevoort described his state of misery and lassitude—"I neither seek to win pleasure or avoid pain"—then begged pardon for "babbling about myself."

My dear Gansevoort, Melville replied on May 29 in a letter he dated June 29, *I look forward to three weeks from now, & think I see you opening this letter in [one] of those pleasant hamlets roundabout London, of which we read in novels.*

Remember that composure of mind is every thing.

I am at the end of my sheet—God bless you My Dear Gansevoort & bring you to your feet again.

Melville added a postscript, written vertically, asking that his brother, who had been instrumental in getting *Typee* published in New York and London, send _every notice of any kind_ of the book.

As Melville wrote this letter on May 29, Gansevoort had been dead for seventeen days.

Gansevoort was his mother's favorite—"the noblest and dearest," according to the Biographer; "the family pride," according to Hardwick.

For fourteen years, from his father's death until his own at age thirty, Gansevoort had felt himself to be financially responsible for the family—
In his final letter to Herman, he wrote that he was living "a life of daily self denial" and that his only remaining desire was to be out of debt.

The family's grief upon Gansevoort's death was compounded by the fact that they could not afford to have his body shipped home.

In his new role as head of the family, Herman wrote letters to President James Polk, Secretary of State James Buchanan, and Secretary of War William Marcy requesting assistance.
Our family are in exceedingly embarrassed circumstances. . . .

His appeal was successful and Gansevoort's body was shipped home on the *Prince Albert* in "a leaden coffin with an appropriate case."

Melville rode twenty hours on a steamer from Albany to New York City, where he transferred his brother's body from the *Prince Albert* to the *Hendrik Hudson*, then sat up with it all night on the return trip up the Hudson River.

He was twenty-six years old.

Until I was twenty-five, I had no development at all, he wrote to Hawthorne as he neared completion of *Moby-Dick.*

He compared himself to a plant grown from an ancient seed taken from a coffin in an Egyptian pyramid—
Like that plant, he had been, since age twenty-five, continuously unfolding.

But I feel that I am now come to the inmost leaf of the bulb, and that shortly the flower must fall to the mould.

A "frighteningly accurate premonition," wrote one scholar, "an elegy to his writing career," written at age thirty-one.

At thirty-one, Melville's life, James Wood wrote at age thirty-one, had been justified.

James Wood is now fifty-four.

The Biographer is eighty-four.

Conor Oberst is forty.

Helen Vendler is eighty-seven.

My husband is forty-nine.

I am forty-nine.

At age thirty-one my husband and I got married in a Shakespeare garden.

Love "is the star to every wand'ring bark," our sole witness read.

We'd gotten engaged quickly, we got married quickly, quickly I quit my job, quickly we packed and left for New Mexico, where my husband had been offered a promising position.

The house we'd rented quickly and from a distance was a squat, dusty shelter, cooled by something called a swamp box.

The unfamiliar scent that permeated the town turned out to be roasting chiles.

Upon our arrival, one of my husband's new colleagues took us to an Applebee's for dinner—
We drank a toast to marriage, a subject he regarded with a kind of reverence.

Everything is magnified in marriage, he told us—
The joy is doubled, and so is the sorrow.

Years later we heard that he'd left his wife, quit his job, and moved with his girlfriend to Eugene.

The best part of our new house was the front porch, where we ate dinner for much of that year.

My husband built a small table out of a wooden pallet; I tried recipes from a manila folder I'd labeled "recipes."

Neighbors said we looked sweet out there in the candlelight, but many nights our conversations turned tense—
Whatever our topic, our topic was in fact the terms of our new marriage.

It was as though we both sensed there was limited time before those terms hardened and set.

After dinner we'd walk Jacob down the street to a park that commemorates women pioneers—
One night it snowed, I remember, and one night we saw a javelina.

In the mornings I'd write poems that were too deliberate and too long, lines trawling toward the margins.

Before leaving for my disposable afternoon job, I'd sometimes type out someone else's poetry to mail to an inmate in Missouri.

A literary journal had mistakenly placed my rejected submission in the inmate's self-addressed stamped envelope, and he had subsequently sent me a letter—
He had recently begun to write poetry, he wrote, and wanted to know how he could improve.

I never gave the inmate advice, but occasionally typed and mailed him a poem selected more or less at random from the books on my desk.

All poems, it began to seem to me, are about imprisonment.

I thought of the inmate recently when I read an interview with Mary Ruefle, who as poet laureate of Vermont intends to send a thousand poems to a thousand randomly chosen citizens of her state.

She began mailing one poem per day during quarantine, selecting names and addresses from her Bennington phone book—
"I thought that this is a perfect time to begin to do it," she said, "with everyone being at home, receptive for getting a poem."

In the interview she mentions just one poem she sent, a haiku by Issa:

> As if nothing had happened—
> the crow,
> and the willow.

One night before everything that's happened happened—March 3, 2019, according to the travel agent's itinerary I just located in an email folder—I picked up Mary Ruefle at the airport.

Presumably we shook hands, as was the custom then.

Her suitcase was large and, if I remember correctly, maroon.

Inside it, I came to learn, was one of the two volumes of *The Melville Log*, a vast compendium of uninterpreted biographical records compiled by Jay Leyda (1910–1988), an avant-garde filmmaker and amateur Melvillean—
"extracts from Melville's letters and from letters written to him; entries in diaries, inscriptions in presentation copies of his books; tax records, publisher's records; items from naval records and newspaper gossip columns; book reviews; and so on, almost *ad infinitum*."

"[Q]uarry," Leyda calls Melville in his introduction.

The *Log* concludes with a rueful epilogue that specifies informational voids left to be filled—
"Perhaps this book should have been more rightly named—*Melville: The Endless Study*," Leyda writes.

I'd never heard of *The Melville Log*.

PS2386.L4.
Durably bound, more royal than navy.

It would appear, my husband once said, that Mary Ruefle is a Melville vector.

If there is ever a Ruefle Log, I happen to have a few items to contribute:
    —a travel itinerary for her residency at the University of
    Cincinnati
    —a small stationery envelope labeled "Mary Ruefle food receipts
    3/3–3/9" with a note indicating that the noodle place could not
    provide her with an itemized receipt
    —a typed letter providing the title and brief description of
    her forthcoming lecture "On Imagination," as well as her
    audiovisual requirements (a compact disc player)

The *y* in her handwritten signature trails down the page to a stamped image of a snail.

Issa, incidentally:

    Under the evening moon
    the snail
        is stripped to the waist.

Translated by Robert Hass.

Who forty years ago said that one of his favorite poems in the world was by Issa:

> Asked how old he was
> the boy in the new kimono
> stretched out all five fingers.

Last night before I fell asleep, or at any rate before I turned out the light, I read a letter written by Elizabeth Hardwick and Robert Lowell's daughter, Harriet.

"I am now fifteen," she wrote to her father, "whatever that means."

He responded by telegram from England that he was "appalled" that he'd forgotten her birthday, that he'd been boasting about her, that the milestone was "glorious," and that he was teaching Donne.

"After a while one *is* older—" he wrote to Elizabeth Hardwick when he was fifty-six, "stiffness, cold fingers and toes."

Their daughter, Harriet, is now sixty-three.

Robert Hass is seventy-nine.

Mary Ruefle is sixty-eight.

Ruefle takes her motto from Henry Miller: "Paint as You Like and Die Happy."

She'd like to read *Anna Karenina* again but not *War and Peace*.
She'd like to read *Moby-Dick* again—

Will she?

"I don't know."

"The things that cannot be done twice!" Lowell wrote to Elizabeth Bishop at age fifty-one.

Five years later, four years before his death, he wrote to her, "It seems unbelievable that I've statistically lived so much much the largest division of my life."

So much much—thus was it written, or thus at least was it transcribed in the collected correspondence of Bishop and Lowell.

"I thought at first that we might have made a transcription error with 'much much,' but it is definitely there in Lowell's very clear typescript," co-editor Thomas Travisano wrote in reply to my inquiry.

He generously attached a photograph of the letter, which was typed on an aerogram.

In this letter Lowell quotes his translation of the Russian proverb that concludes Pasternak's "Hamlet":
"To live a life is not to cross a field."

"We cannot cross the field, only walk it . . ." he elaborated to Bishop, "finishing or not finishing this or that along the way."

As Melville walked the Common on the morning of his wedding to Elizabeth Knapp Shaw, he found a four-leaf clover.

Lucky Melville, one says.

He later presented it to Lizzie, who pressed it between the pages of a family Bible.

(According to family legend, probably apocryphal, Melville gave Lizzie a new four-leaf clover every year on their anniversary.)

They were married in late morning in the presence of about one hundred guests—
"It is all dreamy and indistinct to me—" Lizzie wrote, "a vision of Herman by my side, a confused crowd of rustling dresses, a row of boots, and Mr. Young in full canonicals standing before me, giving utterance to the solemn words of obligation."

According to her younger half brother, she comported herself admirably and "did not cry or anything of that sort."

"Mrs. Herman Melville left, in the afternoon, for Canada via the White Mountains."

"I hardly dare to trust myself to speak of what I felt in leaving home," she wrote to her mother during her honeymoon, and in the following weeks pleaded for letters and news.

To her family she self-consciously signed Elizabeth S. Melville— "Don't it look funny!"

Two months after the wedding, the newlyweds were settled in a row house on Fourth Avenue in Manhattan with Melville's mother, four sisters, brother, and sister-in-law.

"With Herman with me always," Lizzie wrote to her cousin as she prepared for the move, "I can be happy and contented anywhere."

On the other hand: "I'm afraid no place will ever seem to me like dear old crooked Boston."

(Lizzie *Hardwick*, by the way, was not as fond of Boston: "wrinkled, spindly-legged, depleted of nearly all her spiritual and cutaneous oils, provincial, self-esteeming.")

Unaccustomed to married life, Lizzie Melville felt initially as if she were merely visiting the Melvilles—
"The illusion is quite dispelled however when Herman stalks into my room without even the ceremony of knocking, bringing me perhaps a button to sew on, or some such equally romantic occupation."

She frequently had to replace the drawstrings that he yanked out of his drawers while getting undressed.

Other "romantic occupations" included cleaning her husband's study during his morning walk, filling his inkwell, preening his quill pen, listening to his day's work, making fair copies of his manuscripts, and reading to him at night when his eyes were tired.

Most often they stayed home at night so that he was fresh for writing the next morning—
"And it's no sacrifice to me," she wrote to her mother, "for I am quite as contented, and more—to stay at home as long as he will stay with me."

In their first three years of marriage, Melville wrote three novels, plus half of a first draft of *Moby-Dick*.

He composed with "Mozartean speed during his New York years," according to one biographer.

Like Mozart, Melville has been, by some, posthumously diagnosed as manic-depressive—
"In Melville's periods of peak productivity, his work habits were suggestive of hypomania," notes one physician.

Melville's long hours in his study, often without food or drink, caused Lizzie to worry about his health and sanity.

Words he is reported to have spoken repeatedly: "Oh Lizzy! the book!—the book!—what *will* become of the *Book!*"

The book, his third, was *Mardi*, which began as a conventional seafaring story of the sort his publisher wanted, but became, in the words of one biographer, "a fantasy tour of its author's imagination."

Melville explained to his publisher that he began to feel *irked, cramped & fettered* by his fact-based narrative, and longed *to plume [his] pinions for a flight.*

He flew.

"As we proceed, there is some wild writing," reported the advance reader of his British publisher—
One chapter ("Dreams"), she wrote, "could almost seem to have been written by a madman."

In this relentlessly metaphorical chapter, dreams are buffaloes and the narrator is a buffalo hunter.

He is also a frigate and a planet and *an eagle at the world's end* and also eagles' prey.

And my soul sinks down to the depths, and soars to the skies; and comet-like
reels on through such boundless expanses.
Fire flames on my tongue.
The fever runs through me like lava; my hot brain burns like a coal.

You know who else had a hot brain is Robert Lowell, I told my husband.

"His brain was literally hot," Hardwick wrote to Lowell's biographer, describing her husband's manic episodes—
"The breakdowns had the aspect of a 'brain fever,' such as you read about in 19th century fiction," she wrote.

Lowell proposed to Hardwick in a letter written from a hospital where he was being treated for mania—
"How happy we'll be together writing the world's masterpieces, swimming and washing dishes."

He added in a postscript that he was rereading *The Idiot*.

Were they happy? my husband asked.

He was trimming the ears of our dog, whom he had placed upon a card table that had once belonged to my grandmother and at which she had actually played cards.

Somehow the pile of cut hair on the table was as big as the dog.

I knew that it would soon be time for me to feed her treats and speak to her soothingly as he cut around her eyes.

Lowell and Hardwick were happy, I told him, when they weren't miserable.

One critic, I said, called their marriage a Nantucket sleigh ride, a term for the dragging of a whaleboat by a harpooned whale.

In their first four years together, Lowell suffered four major breakdowns, and during their marriage at least ten.

This morning I find Lowell coatless in Harvard Square in January; Lowell standing in the middle of the highway with arms outstretched; Lowell smelling brimstone in the Indiana University faculty club; Lowell holding Allen Tate out a window while reciting "Ode to the Confederate Dead"; Lowell trying to conduct the orchestra at the Metropolitan Opera; Lowell naked, astride an equestrian statue in Buenos Aires; Lowell cabling the pope and Dwight Eisenhower to announce that America was the new Roman Empire; Lowell searching for Etruscan treasures in the walls of his house; Lowell drinking disinfectant and eating detergent; Lowell declaring himself to be King James IV, Caesar, Napoleon, the Virgin Mary; Lowell reading *Mein Kampf,* weeping and declaring that Hitler was a better writer than Melville.

And this morning I find Lowell, Christmas Eve 1966, confronted by eight Boston police officers who had come to take him to McLean.

He threw a milk bottle at them before agreeing to go on the condition that they sit down and listen to him recite "Waking in the Blue," a poem about one of his previous stays in that hospital.

The eight imposing officers sat in the home of Hardwick and Lowell on a snowy Christmas Eve and listened to a poem from *Life Studies,* one of the most consequential volumes in the history of American poetry.

Then they took him away.

"For poetry makes nothing happen," Auden famously wrote.

In his letter supporting Lowell's nomination for the Oxford Poetry Chair, Auden acknowledged that Lowell occasionally "has to go into the bin."

"The warning signals are three a) He announces that he is the *only* living poet b) a romantic and usually platonic attraction to a young girl and c) he gives a huge party."

Hardwick described the cycle in a letter to her lifelong friend Mary McCarthy: "He leaves home, rushes off to another girl, announces that he's in love, and has this manic affair and then he's carted off to the hospital until he is well and then he comes back home."

One of Lowell's worst episodes occurred in early 1954 while he was a poet in residence at the University of Cincinnati—
the same residency, it so happens, held by Mary Ruefle in 2019.

Lowell's lectures became increasingly incoherent, his behavior increasingly bizarre and aggressive—
He spoke, according to one English professor, "like a machine gun with blazing eyes."

The chair of the English Department placed the largest members of his faculty in the front row of Lowell's lectures "in case anything violent developed."

Another risk of the in-person event, said my husband, who would likely have been assigned the front row.

During Lowell's stay in Cincinnati he was in love with an Italian music student—

Before being hospitalized he declared regularly that he intended to divorce Hardwick and marry Giovanna Madonia.

For over twenty years Hardwick endured the humiliation of Lowell's public infidelities while nursing him and managing all practical matters.

On one occasion a jilted lover sent Lowell a stack of bills, which he dropped on the floor—
"I picked them up and paid them," Hardwick told his biographer.

Don't do it, Lizzie!
Don't pay those bills, Lizzie!

But if I stopped her would she still be Hardwick?

"Women, wronged in one way or another," she wrote in her essay "Seduction and Betrayal," "are given the overwhelming beauty of endurance, the capacity for high or lowly suffering, for violent feeling absorbed, finally tranquillized, for the radiance of humility, for silence, secrecy, impressive acceptance."

Hardwick composed this essay on the compelling attributes of the literary heroine roughly two years after Lowell left her for Caroline Blackwood.

Forbearance, independence, grief—
"These are tremendously moving qualities, and when they are called upon it is usual for the heroine to overshadow the man who is the origin of her torment."

According to Dan Chiasson, Hardwick in her marriage to Lowell

developed "forms of self-negation beyond what most of us can even contemplate"—
including an acceptance of Lowell's "girls."

Lowell's infidelities, I told my husband, were mentioned in Hardwick's *New York Times* obituary but not in his.
But Herman Melville, I told him, is mentioned in both.

When Lowell was well, he was, by myriad accounts, gentle, kind, and funny, and particularly good with children and adolescents.

During summers in Maine, he took his daughter on late-night drives to see foxes, porcupines, deer.
He read to her—*Charlotte's Web, Just So Stories, The Hound of the Baskervilles.*
He read his poems to her, and sought her opinion.

"I remember the sound of his voice, his breathing," she said—
"It sounded like waves crashing to me as a child."

"He had that quality, that he could make the dullest thing, like going to pick up the laundry, seem exciting," said Caroline Blackwood.

"He was the most extraordinary person I have ever known," said Elizabeth Hardwick, "like no one else."

"Of course I suffered a good deal in the alliance," she said, "but I very much feel it was the best thing that ever happened to me."

Even after Lowell left her, Hardwick continued to take care of him—
"She did his taxes, arranged the sale of his papers, kept his clothes mothballed and his typewriter in good shape."

When he was hospitalized in 1970 and Caroline fled, Hardwick and a friend flew to London.

She had Lowell's clothes washed, she cut his hair.

And gave him cards with stamped, pre-addressed envelopes so that he would write to their daughter.

"He accepts our efforts like an invalid Archbishop," she wrote to Mary McCarthy, "seeing nothing extraordinary in the service."

During that year McCarthy told Hardwick many times that she was better off without Lowell—

"Everyone insists that I am," Hardwick wrote to Lowell in July 1971— "But can it be true?"

There came a time when Lizzie Melville's family believed she would be better off without her husband.

In May 1867 they devised a plan to extricate her from the marriage: she would travel to Boston, ostensibly for a family visit, then Herman would be notified that "a separation, for the present at least, has been decided on."

Melville at this time was forty-seven, had not published a novel in eleven years, had struggled to publish his poetry, and had recently begun working six days a week as a customs inspector.

In a letter to Lizzie's minister, her half brother wrote that the Melvilles' marriage had been for some years "a cause of anxiety"—
He hoped Reverend Bellows would counsel Lizzie to leave her husband so that "the present lamentable state of things can be ended."

His sister, he wrote, was "convinced that her husband is insane."

(Melville at this time was "not at all insane," according to the Biographer.)

Bellows presented the plan to Lizzie, after which she wrote a letter that thanks him for discussing her "griefs," but gives no indication that she will leave her husband—

"I lay to heart your encouraging words, and pray for submission and faith."

These two letters to Reverend Bellows were discovered in 1975 by Walter D. Kring, and came to be known as the "Kring Find"—"a bombshell" in the world of Melville studies.

Although Melville scholars had long suspected grave difficulties in the Melvilles' marriage, they had had no direct evidence.

These letters were "new and appalling and horrifying," according to the Biographer.
"We all were stunned," said one leading Melville scholar.
"I wasn't shocked," said another, "but I thought, well, here it is."

Some years later, the Melville Society published the letters along with solicited commentary in a booklet titled *The Endless, Winding Way in Melville: New Charts by Kring and Carey*— $847 on Amazon, though I was able to borrow an online copy for one hour at the Internet Archive.

And this morning borrow it again.

In their foreword, the editors, Donald Yannella and the Biographer, write, "We know full well that humane scholars will proceed cautiously and responsibly."

This booklet has no spine.
On which to print its long and misleading title.

It contains anecdotal evidence, derived from family stories and letters, that Melville verbally and physically abused his wife.

According to one oft-repeated story, alluded to in the booklet by Melville's great-grandson, Melville once came home drunk on brandy and threw Lizzie down the stairs—

"All this has been filtered through so many ears and mouths, and minds of such diverse motivation, it is impossible of verification."

"It may not be true at all," wrote Melville's great-grandson.

"On the other hand, worse may be true."

"Who knows?"

The Biographer does:

"He didn't beat his wife."

"Could Herman have brushed Lizzie out of his way as he was going up the stairs and could she have fallen against the wall?" he said to an interviewer.

"It takes so little to get down through the family as an act of violence."

Other commentary in the booklet strives by various means to defend Melville and protect his reputation—

> E.g.: Lizzie's "uncomprehending ordinariness," her lack of
> "intellect, wit and grace."
>
> Lizzie was a "poor housekeeper" and "could not have been an
> easy person to live with."
>
> "Lizzie seems to have had a blend of qualities uniquely
> calculated to grate on Melville's nature."
>
> E.g.: Melville's cruelties were "unpremeditated, almost
> inadvertent."
>
> "Most serious authors are trials to their wives."
>
> "Melville would be the first to admit that he was insane from
> what he called the 'green grocer's' point of view."

The booklet languished spinelessly on the shelves of university libraries for more than a decade until 1994, when a young scholar named Elizabeth Renker published an article in *American Literature* titled "Herman Melville, Wife Beating, and the Written Page"—
"In the pages that follow I will present and review the indications in the historical record that Herman Melville physically and emotionally abused Elizabeth Shaw Melville."

These indications are numerous, though anecdotal.

Or, these indications, though anecdotal, are numerous.

In 1991 Renker had found *The Endless, Winding Way in Melville* "buried on the shelf" in the Ohio State University library—
She was "stunned," "[a]ngry," "irritated."

Initially she thought the booklet was a cover-up orchestrated by influential Melvilleans, though she's come to regard it as evidence not of deception but of denial—
"It had a lot more to do with the kinds of emotional investments scholars made in Melville."

Renker cried while reading from *Moby-Dick* at her wedding, though this morning I can't determine whether that occurred before or after she found *The Endless, Winding Way* in the stacks during her first year as a professor at Ohio State.

"It looks like there aren't any great matches for your search."

Renker's article in *American Literature* "stirred a tempest" and "lathered" Melvilleans:
They charged her with making speculative leaps based on flimsy evidence.

The editor of the Melville Society journal called her "wrongheaded and guided by a kind of moldy feminist assumption."

"I did not let my old Melville go without pain," she said, "but I saw right away that this new understanding of his troubled life is truer."

The Biographer, who does not, it appears, cite Renker or her work, concludes his two-thousand-page Melville biography with Melville's wife—
"Marrying him did not seem the worst thing she ever did."

I put Volume 2 back beneath my laptop where it serves as ergonomic hack/Zoom aid.

It's too heavy to read comfortably in bed, I've found—
3.45 pounds, according to Amazon.

For recumbent readers I recommend Andrew Delbanco's *Melville: His World and Work* (1.88 pounds) or Laurie Robertson-Lorant's *Melville: A Biography* (2.4 pounds).

Or, of course, Hardwick's *Herman Melville* (10.4 ounces), which I finished once again last night.

Are you awake? I asked my husband, hoping he would awake.

Hardwick ends her biography with resignation and reconciliation— with Lizzie's care for Melville "in his great distress and need," and his apparent gratitude "for her long years as Mrs. Melville."

On the question of abuse, she says only that Melville was "given to violence in the household."

We'll probably never know, I would have said to my husband if he had woken.

He was protected from me by the sound of my fan and the mound of covers I had flung between us.

"You hear a lot about hot flashes, but hot flashes are the least of it," wrote Mary Ruefle in an essay about menopause.

This essay reproduces a "cryalog" that she kept around the time of her forty-sixth birthday.

"Fri Cx1 very bad"
"Sat Cx4 very bad"
"W Cx1 a little"

Only seven of the fifty-eight days in the cryalog are marked "NC," which means she did not cry.
The most she cried in one day, a Thursday, was five times ("CCCCC").
Her longest crying streak was twenty-three days.

During menopause, Ruefle writes, "A kind of wild forest blood runs in your veins"—
You may want to abandon your partner, walk out of the country, steal things, crash your car, drink vinegar, "fuck a tree."

You might, she writes, "take up an insane and hopeless cause."

You might, for example, take up the American author Herman Melville.
You might in your fiftieth year conduct an audit of the Justified Life.

Would I be turning on my book light to read about Melville in the middle of the night if I knew for certain that he beat his wife?

That he threw her down the stairs?

I do know that Robert Lowell broke his first wife's nose.

(Person A punches his wife and writes great poems . . .)

"What some people want is for me to produce a letter in which Melville said, 'I'm still beating my wife,' and that I can't do," said Renker.

"With abuse victims, their skeletons often show it," said Dr. William Meredith in a discussion with a Melvillean about the controversy.

"They could dig up the wife," he said—
"They could look at the skeleton."

Dr. Meredith is not a medical doctor or a forensic scientist, but a musicologist.

As director of the Ira F. Brilliant Center for Beethoven Studies at San Jose State University, he has been tangentially involved in scientific analysis of Beethoven's remains.

The Brilliant Center possesses a portion of a lock of Beethoven's hair purchased at auction for £3,600 in 1994—a steal, according to one prominent hair collector.

The lock contains hair of three colors: brown, gray, and white—
"I remember thinking it was very beautiful when I saw it," said Dr. Meredith.

By the time Beethoven was buried he was almost bald because so many admirers had cut locks of his hair—
The one in the Brilliant Center was taken by a fifteen-year-old composer the day after Beethoven's death.

This morning I see that a lock of hair purportedly belonging to Emily Dickinson, and once part of the estate of the poet James Merrill, is for sale on eBay for $450,000—
It has thirty-five watchers, not including me.

The lock sold at auction last year for just $800 because its provenance could not be traced beyond Merrill, who as a young man may or may not have broken into the Dickinson house and taken the hair, along with a sherry glass.

"My Hair is bold, like the Chestnut Bur," Dickinson once wrote—
"and my eyes, like the Sherry in the Glass, that the Guest leaves."

Another lock of Dickinson's hair, this one with "undisputed provenance," is in the special collections of Frost Library at Amherst College.

At age twenty-two she sent the hair to a friend in a letter—
"I shall never give you anything again that will be half so full of sunshine as this wee lock of hair," she wrote.

The wee lock is coiled like a nest, surprisingly red.

Stored in a piece of folded paper inside a cloth-covered box—
Burgundy, if I remember correctly.

One day—this was during the Bad Time, when I felt marooned in my marriage—my husband and children searched for four-leaf clovers on the college quad, while I descended to the archives, sat at a wood table opposite the standing archivist, and stared at Emily Dickinson's hair.

"Why does the writing make us chase the writer?" asks the narrator of Julian Barnes's novel *Flaubert's Parrot*— "Why aren't the books enough?"

After several minutes, I rose from the table, thanked the archivist, and said I hoped I hadn't taken up too much of his time.

"You'd be surprised," he told me, "how long some people stay."

It so happens that a lock of hair is among the items collected in the Herman Melville papers housed at Harvard's Houghton Library—
labeled "a lock of Toby's hair," and dated 1846.

The hair belonged to Richard Tobias Greene, Melville's shipmate on the whaler *Acushnet*, and his companion during many of the adventures recounted in Melville's first book, *Typee*.

After a year and a half at sea, and increasingly disgruntled with conditions on the *Acushnet*, Melville decided to abandon ship in the Marquesas Islands—
He was, according to Geoffrey O'Brien, an "instinctive escape artist."

As Melville recounts in *Typee*, he had resolved to tell no one of his plan, until one night on deck when he saw a shipmate *plunged in a profound reverie*—
Toby, who had *a mind of deep passion* and *a remarkably prepossessing exterior.*

The two men *had battled out many a long watch together, beguiling the weary hours with chat, song, and story.*

Melville's narrator invites Toby to join his escape, and as Toby proves *ripe for the enterprise*, the two men make plans and shake hands—
We then ratified our engagement with an affectionate wedding of palms.

As was the custom, then.

While on shore leave, Melville and Toby fled into the mountains, survived for days in the wet jungle, then made a treacherous descent to a valley where they lived with a friendly tribe of cannibals, until one day Toby left to greet incoming ships and never returned.

Melville, fearing he would be eaten, eventually escaped onto an Australian whaler.

He joined a mutiny, he escaped imprisonment in Tahiti, he broke an indenture in Hawaii, he enlisted in the U.S. Navy.

After fourteen months aboard the USS *United States*, a crowded and oppressive ship on which he witnessed five deaths and one hundred and sixty-three floggings, he was discharged in Boston.

He was twenty-five—
Nearly four years had elapsed since he took to sea on the *Acushnet*, owing money to his landlady and a shoemaker.

He was discharged on October 14, I told my husband, but didn't leave for New York to see his family until October 19.

All Elizabeth Hardwick has to say about this gap is that he was "lingering or malingering."

The Biographer thinks it is likely that he visited the Shaws, and likely that he made "a sensational impression" on Lizzie, his future wife, and likely that as he found his land legs he "more or less unconsciously combined athleticism with eroticism in his gait," but he admits that there is no documentary evidence.

Nobody really knows what he was doing during these days, I told my husband, or those days, rather.

Maybe he was drinking champagne, I said.
Or eating until his pants no longer fit.
Maybe he was with women, or with men.
Maybe he had trouble saying goodbye to naval officer Jack Chase, whom he would commemorate in *White-Jacket* and to whom he would dedicate *Billy Budd* decades later.
Maybe he was browsing bookstores, though he was not yet the bibliophile he would become.
Liberated on land, maybe he was just walking the city.

Athletically and erotically, my husband said.

Maybe he just wasn't ready to see his family yet.
Maybe he wanted to be alone.

The USS *United States*, I told my husband, was not quite twice as large as the *Acushnet* but had almost twenty times as many sailors.

I told him that the men slept in hammocks that were eighteen inches apart.

There's this part in *White-Jacket*, I said, where he calls a hammock a stew-pan, where *you can almost hear yourself hiss*.

His mom's house, though, I said, would have been another stew-pan.

I told him that Melville's mother is reported to have made her eight children sit silently on stools around her bed while she took her daily nap.

We decided to grant Melville his five private days in Boston.

Sometimes it's best to leave the blanket over the birdcage, my husband said idiomatically, although that is not in fact an idiom, I see this morning.

When Melville finally made it to his mother's house in Lansingburgh, New York—"sunburned, bearded, and rugged as a bear"—his adventures, as well as his notable gifts as a storyteller, made him "a celebrity of sorts."

Having been encouraged to record his stories, he wrote *Typee* in his mother's attic—
or, having moved a large desk down from his mother's attic, he wrote *Typee* before an upstairs window with a view of the Hudson—
or, he wrote *Typee* at his brothers' law office in Manhattan where there was a plentiful supply of paper and pens.

Wherever he wrote his travelogue, he finished it in about six months, after which he received a "devastating rejection" from the Harper brothers' publishing house, whose editors did not believe the book's events could be true.

According to the Biographer, Melville maintained a "lifelong bitterness" toward the Harpers.

But Gansevoort, months before he died in London at age thirty, proved able to find a British and then an American publisher, and Melville's first book appeared in early 1846.

Typee garnered enthusiastic reviews and appreciative readers, including Nathaniel Hawthorne, Henry Wadsworth Longfellow, Bronson Alcott, Henry David Thoreau, Margaret Fuller, and Walt Whitman.

Religious presses, however, objected to risqué descriptions of natives and critical portrayals of missionaries, and some reviewers accused Melville of exaggeration and fabrication.

Melville defended himself to the editor of the Albany *Argus*, which subsequently ran an editorial, likely written by Melville himself— *The author desires to state to the public, that Typee is a true narrative of events which actually occurred to him.*

Although there may be moving incidents and hairbreadth escapes, it is scarcely more strange than such as happen to those who make their home on the deep.

Melville was not quite truthful on the subject of his truthfulness— e.g., he stayed three weeks with the cannibals, whereas his narrator remained in their village for four months.

According to one biographer, "It is difficult to know how much of what Melville describes in *Typee* is pure imagination, how much is wishful thinking, and how much is fact."

A house and sign painter in Buffalo, having read a disparaging review of the book in the New York *Evangelist*, wrote a letter to the Buffalo *Commercial Advertiser* attesting to the veracity of the work.

Toby!

The former shipmates and deserters had not known what became of one another in the four years since they separated in the Marquesas.

The editor of the Albany *Argus*, who exchanged copies of his paper with other editors across the state, saw Toby's letter in the Buffalo paper and forwarded it to Melville, who wrote immediately to Toby to arrange a meeting.

Little is known about Melville's meeting with Toby in Rochester in July 1846, though presumably Toby reported that his sister had named her son in honor of Melville:
Richard Melville Hair, born 1843.

We do know that Melville procured two items of corroborative and perhaps sentimental value: a portrait of Toby and a lock of his hair.

He wrote to his British publisher, *I have seen Toby. have his dargurr-type—a lock of those ebon curls.*
The lock that is now preserved in Harvard's Houghton Library.

Years later, Toby named his own son after Melville:
Herman Melville Greene, born 1854.

Oliver Russ, another former shipmate of Melville's, on whom the character of Nord in *White-Jacket* is based, *also* named his son after Melville:
Herman Melville Russ, born mostly likely 1847.

Good thing, my husband said from the peninsula, that we didn't have a son.

One night *during a profoundly quiet midnight watch*, the narrator of *White-Jacket* and Nord *scoured all the prairies of reading; dived into the bosoms of authors, and tore out their hearts.*

The narrator proclaims that that night he *learned more than he has ever done in any single night since.*

Russ wrote a letter to Melville fifteen years after they sailed together on the naval frigate the USS *United States*—
"Now what I wish to say is that I in the course of the next year after our return from sea I took to wife one of the fair daughters of the state of Maine and in two years from that day a son was born to us a substancial token of our mutual love and to manifest the high regard in which I have ever held yourself I named him Herman Melville Russ at that time I did not expect ever to hear of you again or that you would be numbered among the literary writers of the day."

Russ expressed his hope that Melville might send his son "some present as a keepsake."

In late 1860 Melville decided to send engraved silver spoons to all three of his namesakes: Herman Melville Russ, Herman Melville Greene, and Richard Melville Hair.

All three of these spoons are unlocated—
"For the Melvillean the spoons naturally stir the hope that, when they are found, some paper with the familiar daunting Melville handwriting will be wrapped around them or reposing in a box with them."

The spoon sent to Richard Melville Hair, one Melvillean writes, "must be somewhere out there like a note in a bottle bobbing on a mid-ocean wave."

Melville sent these gifts at a time when he had four children and no income.

He was forty-one years old and finished as a prose writer.
Having proven unsuccessful on the lecture circuit—e.g., "If the lecture was faulty, the delivery can hardly be said to have been less so"—

he imagined he might make a living by writing poetry, though only one American poet could be said to have done so.

Longfellow, my husband guessed, correctly.

In making a gift of the engraved spoons, Melville, as the Biographer notes, "found himself depriving his own family in order to make the magnanimous gesture Russ expected."

At the time he sent the spoons Melville was supposed to be at sea, not at home.

Eight months earlier, his younger brother Tom, the captain of a clipper ship, invited him on a year-long voyage around the world, past Cape Horn to San Francisco, then on to the Far East—
"Much to the family's relief, Herman jumped at the chance," writes one biographer.

Lizzie's father, suspecting that Lizzie "needed a vacation from her demanding and difficult husband," offered Melville his encouragement and support.

And a deal: in exchange for debt forgiveness Melville transferred ownership of his farm to his father-in-law, who then deeded it to Lizzie for one dollar.

In the month between Tom's invitation and their departure, Melville prepared a volume of his poetry for publication.

He left a manuscript for Lizzie to copy, and for his other brother, Allan, he composed memoranda *concerning the publication of my verses—*
twelve enumerated stipulations, including *Don't have the Harpers*; *The*

sooner the thing is printed and published, the better; Dont have any clap-trap announcements and "sensation" puffs; For God's sake don't have By the author of "Typee" "Piddledee" &c on the title-page; Let the title-page be simply,

Poems

by

Herman Melville.

He concluded: *Of all human events, perhaps, the publication of a first volume of verses is the most insignificant; but though a matter of no moment to the world, it is still of some concern to the author,—as these Mem. show— Pray therefore, don't laugh at my Mem. but give heed to them, and so oblige*

Your brother

Herman—

With the copied manuscript Lizzie forwarded two additional requests that Melville, in his haste, had forgotten: that the book be plainly bound and that the publishers not use a blue and gold binding, which was fashionable at that time.

Melville departed on the *Meteor* on May 30, 1860, with the expectation that he would soon be a published poet and the hope that the voyage would be good for his health.

The trip, however, was not entirely restorative— e.g., prolonged bad weather and seasickness, a collision with a ship whose captain had fallen asleep, a harrowing winter passage around Cape Horn.

On August 9 a young sailor fell from the main topsail, struck his head on a spar, and died instantly— *the body bled incessantly & up to the moment of burying*, Melville recorded in his journal.

The next day he wrote, *But little sorrow to the crew—all goes on as usual—I, too, read & think, & walk & eat & talk, as if nothing had happened—as if I did not know that death is indeed the King of Terrors.*

This was his final journal entry on the trip.

Melville spent much of this journey studying the "small library" of poetry he had brought with him—
His reading aboard the *Meteor* suggests that he had begun to aspire to write epic poetry.

In his copy of the New Testament he underlined a passage in Romans 14: "Hast thou faith? have *it* to thyself before God."
The only kind of Faith—one's own, he wrote in the top margin.

Upon reaching San Francisco four and a half months after departing from Boston, Melville and his brother went to the harbormaster to collect their mail.

Tom learned that instead of sailing to the Far East he was to transport wheat back around Cape Horn to England.

Herman learned that he was not a published poet—
His friends and family had been unable to find a publisher.

In her husband's absence Lizzie seemed to take on his frustration and bitterness regarding the literary market—
"I suppose that if John Milton were to offer 'Paradise Lost' to the Harpers tomorrow," she wrote to one of Melville's literary friends, "it would be promptly rejected as 'unsuitable' not to say, denounced as dull."

According to the Biographer, the rejection of Melville's poetry came as "a violent psychological blow" that induced him to cut short his voyage with Tom.

After sending Lizzie a letter via Pony Express informing her that he was coming home, Melville sailed to Panama on the *Cortes*, crossed the isthmus by rail, and returned home as a first-class passenger on the *North Star*.

The Pony Express letter would have cost at least five dollars, or $156.86 today; the first-class passage cost more than he had earned in the last two years.

The *Berkshire County Eagle* announced his imminent early homecoming, noting that "Mr. Melville's health is better in some particulars than when he left home, but we regret to learn that he has not experienced the full benefit hoped from the trip."

It's possible that Melville cut his trip short not because of his health or his dashed expectations of publication but, as one biographer suggests, because he was homesick.

One afternoon on the deck of the *Meteor*, he had made a drawing of his homecoming, as if witnessed from a remote and elevated vantage.

He sketched his farmhouse, his barn, his orchard, his pasture, his woodlot, his flag, his fence.

(All, strictly speaking, now belonging to his wife.)

In the foreground, not immediately discernible, three small figures stand in the road before an approaching horse and carriage—
It is to be supposed, he annotated, *that I am in the carriage; & the figures are welcoming me.*

He was particularly proud of his rendering of his horse, Charlie.

He wrote letters, addressed from *Pacific Ocean*, to Lizzie and two of their children.

The letter to Lizzie is unlocated, but the letters to his children are in the Herman Melville papers at Harvard.
Along with a wing of a flying fish that he enclosed for his daughter Fanny, age five.

Undigitized, alas.

He wrote to Fanny's older sister, Bessie, age seven, about the birds that had followed the ship for days—
They never see any orchards, and have a taste of the apples & cherries, like your gay little friend in Pittsfield Robin Red Breast Esq.

He supposes, he wrote, that she's been going on walks and picking strawberries.

I hope you take good care of little FANNY and that when you go on the hill, you go this way:
(Here he drew Bessie and her sister as tiny figures walking up a hill, holding hands.)

[T]hat is to say, hand in hand.

"This tender sketch of his two daughters walking up a hill justifies Melville's life," according to not anyone at all.

By–by
Papa.

His much longer letter to his oldest child, Malcolm, age eleven, is signed, *Your affectionate father / H Melville.*

He wrote to Malcolm about the *Meteor*'s route and suggested he follow along on a globe—
so you get Mama to clean it off for you.

He described the prolonged bad weather, the death of the sailor at Cape Horn and his burial at sea.

This sailor's name was Ray.
He had a friend among the crew; and they were both going to California, and thought of living there; but you see what happened.

He reminded Malcolm to be obedient and helpful—
Now is the time to show what you are—whether you are a good, honorable boy, or a good-for-nothing one.

The photograph he had of Malcolm and his three siblings he would look at *till the faces almost seem real.*

This morning I was once again denied access to "Some Psychological Reflections on the Death of Malcolm Melville" in the Winter 1976 issue of *Suicide and Life-Threatening Behavior*, so I stared out the window for a while.

So I reread the so-called "Malcolm Letter," written by an exuberant Melville on the occasion of Malcolm's birth—
I think of calling him Barbarossa—Adolphus—Ferdinand—Otho— Grandissimo Hercules—Sampson—Bonaparte—Lambert.

So I electronically consented to my child's remote participation in Freedom from Chemical Dependency Week.

So I ordered more masks, more disinfectant wipes, more birdseed.

So I ordered more dog food and more coffee filters.

So I went to the basement to move the laundry and watched my husband affix a piece of wood to another piece of wood with screws and glue and the appearance of deep contentment.

So I took out the recycling and then the compost.

So I threw the ball for the dog.

So I compared various translations of a haiku about the cold voice of the autumn wind speaking through a crack in the door.

So I regarded a yellow sticky note on which I had at some point written the name of Melville's brother's clipper ship, *Meteor.*

So I noticed an anagram—*remote.*

And another—*emoter.*

So I reread the letters the remote emoter wrote aboard the *Meteor*— There's this great part in the one to Malcolm where Melville explains how the letter will be carried from San Francisco to *a place called Panama* to Havana to New York and finally to Pittsfield.

It will take about twenty-five days, he told his son.

The truth is, Melville's periodic and extended absences from home were likely a welcome respite for Lizzie and their four children.

By numerous accounts he was prone to angry and tyrannical episodes—"ugly attacks," in the phrase of Lizzie's cousin.

His granddaughter years later wrote of his "desperate irascibility" and "bursts of nervous anger."

Of "the solace of brandy."

"Even when he was in a good mood," writes one biographer, "the force of his personality and his need to be the center of attention put enormous demands on others, and when he was in a bad mood, he could be a terror."

Even the Biographer makes reference to "a harsh impoverished household."

The misery and tyranny in the house reached a tragic climax in 1867, which has been called Melville's *annus horribilis*.

In August of the previous year he had published his first book in nearly a decade—
Battle-Pieces and Aspects of the War, a collection of poems and commentary about the Civil War.

Based on his lofty subject matter and the success of other contemporary collections, Melville hoped to achieve a wide readership, make money, and reestablish his literary prestige.

> Melville, Herman (1819–1891):
> hopes of,

"[A] small slither of hope," in the words of one of my husband's students.

[Sic] but evocative.

> "Hope" is the thing that slithers—
> That lurches from its hole—
> Occasions tighter Breathing—
> Then can't be found—at all—

Battle-Pieces received poor reviews and did not sell well.

Melville lost money on the publication, and not long after its release contacted an acquaintance, the collector of customs for the Port of New York, about a job.

In December, less than four months after the publication of his first collection of poetry, he was sworn in as a customs inspector— deputy inspector No. 75.

His salary was $1,200, considerably less than a jailkeeper's.

Based on passing mentions in family letters and their own assumptions about the value of work, early biographers speculated that Melville's job improved his emotional health and thus the atmosphere of his home.

But the Kring Find letters from May 1867, revealing the plot to extricate Lizzie from her marriage, forced reappraisal.

The letters show that "his mood worsened," wrote one scholar.

"It was probably inevitable that Melville's frustration and resentment at what his life had become would spill over into his relationship with his family," wrote another—
"It was the family who were made to feel the force of his dissatisfaction, if only as the luckless crew who slept below him as he paced his quarter-deck."

The luckless crew.

Some facts are these:

1. One night in September 1867, Malcolm Melville, age eighteen, went out with friends.

2. And came home at 3 a.m.

3. His mother, who had waited up, did not scold him.

4. Malcolm apologized and told her that it wouldn't happen again.

5. He kissed his mother and went to bed.

6. In the morning he did not get up for his job at an insurance agency.

7. When one of his sisters called to him he answered, but he never came downstairs.

8. Before leaving for his custom house duties, Malcolm's father suggested that they let Malcolm sleep and face the consequences at work.

9. During the day Malcolm's mother called for him and knocked but he did not reply.

10. That evening Malcolm's father came home late from work.

11. He broke into Malcolm's room.

12. He saw his son lying in his bed.

13. On his left side, in "a semi-fetal position."

14. With "a pistol in his right hand."

15. And "a bullet hole in his right temple."

(16. Mackey, they called him.)

A luckless crew: "the eldest, Malcolm, dead by his own hand; Stanwix, 'possessed with a demon of *restlessness*,' according to his mother, and dead at 35; Elizabeth, an invalid crippled with arthritis to the extent that a doctor once suggested that her fingers be straightened '*by force*'; and Frances, the only child to marry, who late in life would not hear the name of her father spoken."

"It's brutal," writes Robert Hass, "the way some lives / Seem to work and some don't."

Malcolm's death, I told my husband late last night, was initially reported a suicide, but Melville's brother-in-law convinced the coroner to change the cause of death to an accident.

His funeral was held at the Melville home.

I knew Lizzie dressed the body but I kept that to myself.

Oﾠne hot day in the summer of 1872, a newlywed couple at home on Fifty-Third Street in Manhattan received a visit from a bearded man, approximately fifty years old, of indeterminate height.

The visitor had reason to believe that the couple was in possession of a framed and inscribed photograph of his deceased son, a National Guard volunteer—
And indeed, the photograph of the young man in regimental uniform was situated prominently on the mantelpiece of the newlyweds' parlor.

As it was customary at the time for patriotic middle-class Americans to display images of soldiers, even those unknown to them, the couple had recently purchased the photograph at a secondhand store.

The bearded visitor had brought with him a framed watercolor, and he asked the newlyweds if they might consider an exchange.

The couple consented, and the visitor left with the photograph of his dead son and with a bearing that was elsewhere described as upright, nearly military.

Later that day, Lizzie Melville wrote to her husband's cousin that their search had been a success—
"We have the much wished for picture of our dear boy."

The Melvilles had tracked the photograph from Albany, where it had been sent, along with other items, when Malcolm's National Guard regiment had been disbanded.

In the days following Malcolm's death, Herman and Lizzie offered the photograph as a gift to Malcolm's volunteer unit, members of which had served as pallbearers—
The Biographer speculates that "looking on Malcolm's image seemed unbearable" to them.

After the funeral, Melville was granted a week off from work, during which he and Lizzie returned to Arrowhead, now owned by his brother Allan.

Seventeen years had elapsed since Melville had surprised the family by buying the house and farm.

Since he had ridden a horse in the moonlight to tell the Hawthornes that he would be their neighbor, that he would build a tower.

Seventeen years ago, at age thirty-one, "he was on the cusp of an *annus mirabilis*," according to one scholar, "one that would culminate with the publication of *Moby-Dick*."

In early October of that year Melville moved into his new house with his mother, three sisters, Lizzie, and baby Malcolm.

Their first fall on the farm was lovely.

"I never before fully realized the glorious beauty of an October in the country," Augusta wrote to her friend—
"cloudless skies & the balmiest of air—windows & doors all open."

On the evening of October 6, 1850, in his first letter from Arrowhead,

Melville reported to a friend, *It has been a most glowing & Byzantine day—the heavens reflecting the tints of the October apples in the orchard. You should see the maples—you should see the young perennial pines.*

For weeks that fall Melville worked outdoors—
plowing fields, splitting wood, tending animals, harvesting apples.

Every thing to be done, & scarcely any one to help me do it.
But I trust that before a great while we shall be all "to rights," and I shall take my ease on mine mountain.

By taking his ease he presumably meant locking himself in his new study to resume work on a novel about whale hunting.

By Thanksgiving he was sufficiently immersed in the book that he did not join Lizzie and Malcolm on their trip to Boston, where they remained until January 1.

But there were still chores and distractions at home.

Because he wouldn't allow the women to drive the horse and wagon, he had to take them on their errands and visits.

And because his second-floor study was the largest room at Arrowhead, he had to allow them to use it to entertain family during the holiday.

They fed ten people on a stormy day—
"Herman offering his arm to Aunt Mary, led the way,—the tribe of Melville following one by one, up that stairs of many angles," Augusta later reported.

"Everything was beautifully cooked, & every one beautifully happy."

It so happens that this Thursday is Thanksgiving—
Under the circumstances, the CDC recommends celebrating "virtually or with members of your own household."

One member of our household wants to know if we can still dress up (yes).
Another wants to know if she can try wine (maybe).

The complicated, non-traditional dessert my husband will have chosen to make will disappoint him in some way, though it will be very good.

In the evening we'll zoom the distant elders, sheltered in place.

Then play a game—
Boggle, perhaps, or Ticket to Ride.

(In the Boggle box, the foxed lists of words in my grandmother's cursive.)

On Thanksgiving 1850 the Melville tribe played a fortune-telling game called "Home Oracles," with Augusta in the role of seer.

Tea at 7, eggnog at 9—
Their guests "begged they might not be asked to partake of anything more, even if it were Thanksgiving."

This was, I see this morning, thirteen years before Lincoln established the fourth Thursday of November as a national holiday—
"In the midst of a civil war of unequalled magnitude and severity," Lincoln proclaimed, "the American people should take some time for gratitude."

Up to that point, Thanksgiving had been celebrated on different days by individual states, primarily in the North.

Days before he issued his proclamation, Lincoln received a letter from writer and editor Sarah Josepha Hale, imploring him to create a national holiday of thanks—
For thirty-six years she had been lobbying officials about this issue.

Hale, I see, decided to pursue a literary career as a way to support her five children after her husband died—
There were "very few employments in which females can engage with any hope of profit, and my own constitution and pursuits, made literature appear my best resource," she explained.

She published nearly fifty books in her lifetime, I told my husband as we convened in the kitchen to make stuffing and broccoli-cheddar casserole.

Were they any good? he asked.

I don't know, I said, but she wrote "Mary Had a Little Lamb."

That's one of the handwashing songs, one of our daughters said.

My husband said he thought "Mary Had a Little Lamb" was the first thing Edison recorded on his phonograph.

He asked our daughters to just please come over here and take a look at the way they had loaded the dishwasher.

One daughter said that on her field trip to the Ford Museum she had seen Thomas Edison's last breath in a test tube.

My husband said, That doesn't sound right.

I'm not going to get to take that field trip, said her sister, who everyone knows never wanted to take that field trip.

She began to sing "Mary Had a Little Lamb."

I thought my husband was consulting the stuffing recipe on his phone, but he was looking at images of the test tube containing Edison's last breath.

That trip isn't that great, our daughter said, but you get to go on the Rosa Parks bus.

She asked her sister to stop singing but she wouldn't.

Mary had a little lamb, little lamb, little lamb.
Mary had a little lamb, its fleece was white as snow.

[S]now-white was Ahab's ivory leg.
And snow-white, Moby Dick's brow and hump.

It was the whiteness of the whale that above all things appalled me.
There yet lurks an elusive something in the innermost idea of this hue, which strikes more of panic to the soul than that redness which affrights in blood.

"Doom! Doom! Doom!" according to D. H. Lawrence.

According to Lawrence, Melville "knew his race was doomed."
"His white soul, doomed."
"His great white epoch, doomed."

"What I am suggesting," Toni Morrison said of Melville in a lecture delivered in 1988, "is that he was overwhelmed by the philosophical and metaphysical inconsistencies of an extraordinary and unprecedented idea that had its fullest manifestation in his own time in his own country, and that that idea was the successful assertion of whiteness as ideology."

"Melville takes on the concept of evil," according to Yusef Komunyakaa—
"he shows us that whiteness is a map of obsession."

White Ahab hunting whiteness.

Doomed.

"If the Great White Whale sank the ship of the Great White Soul in 1851," Lawrence asked in an essay published in 1923, "what's been happening ever since?"

"Post mortem effects, presumably."

What's been happening ever since Lawrence asked what's been happening ever since?

And everywhere that Mary went the lamb was sure to go.

I have written a wicked book, Melville wrote to Hawthorne, *and feel spotless as the lamb.*

"What does it feel like, one wonders," asked Walker Percy, "to have written *Moby-Dick*?"

Friends, hold my arms! exclaims Ishmael.
For in the mere act of penning my thoughts of this Leviathan, they weary

me, and make me faint with their outreaching comprehensiveness of sweep, as if to include the whole circle of the sciences, and all the generations of whales, and men, and mastodons, past, present, and to come, with all the revolving panoramas of empire on earth, and throughout the whole universe, not excluding its suburbs.

"[A]n elation of freedom and passion," according to Elizabeth Hardwick, as well as "a violent submersion near to drowning."

"[A] triumphant taking-on of hell and coming through," according to Walker Percy.

"[A]n unabated frenzy of inspiration," according to Paul Auster.

"[A]n all-involving and psychically corrosive experience," according to Nathaniel Philbrick.

As for David Gilbert, he cannot hold the book "without feeling the vertiginous swell of its creation."

"Been rereading *Moby-Dick* again," wrote Ralph Ellison in a letter to Albert Murray, "and appreciating for the first time what a truly good time Melville was having when he wrote it."

The book, Ellison noted, "is pervaded by the spirit of play, like real jazz sounds when a master is manipulating it."
"The thing's full of riffs, man."

According to Walker Percy, "The happiness of Melville in *Moby-Dick* is the happiness of the artist discovering, breaking through into the freedom of his art."

In this novel, Percy writes, "Everything works."
"One kills six birds with every stone."

"The problem of meaning ceases to trouble him because he can mean everything at the same time," according to Geoffrey O'Brien—
"All at once Melville knows that he cannot make a false step."

In December 1850, though, Melville wrote in a letter that *taking a book off the brain, is akin to the ticklish & dangerous business of taking an old painting off a panel—you have to scrape off the whole brain in order to get at it with due safety—& even then, the painting may not be worth the trouble.*

He wrote the letter by candlelight, one eye shut and the other squinting—
By the end of his day's work he couldn't see well, and spent his evenings *in a sort of mesmeric state.*

The family occasionally played backgammon or whist, but most often read aloud by the hearth—
That winter they read *David Copperfield.*

(As did the Hawthornes—of her husband's reading, Sophia wrote, "It is better than any acting or opera.")

Initially Melville's writing day ended at 2:30, when, as instructed, one of the women in the house knocked on his study door until he rose from his desk.

While he wrote, they cooked, composed letters, completed chores, cared for Malcolm, and copied Melville's pages.

They looked forward to being taken to the post office in the village by wagon or sleigh—

"We visit the post office with such interest every eve^g & are so disappointed if there is nothing for us," wrote Augusta.

But as the winter progressed Melville extended his writing day.

Lizzie later recalled that he "would sit at his desk all day not eating any thing till four or five o clock—then ride to the village after dark."

"When dinner trays were brought up in the evening," said Jay Leyda, author of *The Melville Log*, "the lunch trays would still be there."

In January, Melville, increasingly frustrated and angry when his work was interrupted, capitulated to the women's repeated requests to be allowed to drive the wagon.

"As you may imagine we are all highly delighted at the idea of being able to drive off whenever we have an inclination to taste the fresh air," Augusta wrote to one of her sisters—
"Now we shall be quite independent."

On January 22 Melville decided to visit Hawthorne for the first time since he moved to Arrowhead.

He drove the wagon through snow, "six miles of rutted, jolting road." And brought with him his shaggy black Newfoundland, whose name—a tip of the hat to the Biographer—I've just this morning discovered.

(Major.)

It was likely during this visit that the Hawthorne children showed Melville the grave of a bird they had found dead in the bough of a fir tree.

They hoped it would come back to life in the spring.

Melville was welcomed, fed cold chicken, and given two of Haw-thorne's books: *Twice-Told Tales* and, for Malcolm, *Grandfather's Chair*.

Three weeks later, Melville wrote to a friend that the stories in *Twice-Told Tales* were even better than those in *Mosses from an Old Manse*.

He marked the following passage in a story called "The Gentle Boy": "'Friend,' replied the little boy, in a sweet, though faltering voice, 'they call me Ilbrahim, and my home is here.'"

Jay Leyda suggests that this sentence may have influenced the famous first line of *Moby-Dick*.

Margaret Atwood's favorite first line—
"Why Ishmael?" she wrote in a tweet.
"It's not his real name. Who's he speaking to? Eh?"

"A second before this person was likely a John or a Philip, a Henry," wrote David Gilbert, who also names *Call me Ishmael* as his favorite first line.

"Call me Jonah," begins Kurt Vonnegut's *Cat's Cradle*.
"Call me Smitty," begins Philip Roth's *The Great American Novel*.
"Call me Monk," culminates the opening paragraph of Percival's Everett's *Erasure*.

"My name is Ruth," begins Marilynne Robinson's *Housekeeping*, which she calls her "Moby-Jane."

"We both drowned a lot of people," Robinson told an interviewer, laughing.

The opening paragraph of the first chapter of *Moby-Dick* is, according to Ta-Nehisi Coates, "the greatest paragraph in any work of fiction, at any point, in all of history."
"And not just human history, but galactic and extra-terrestrial history too."

"Do not come to me with your drab and sorry works which I have not read."
"Melville desecrates their temples, steals their horses, and howls among the lamentation!"

"Damn right. Melville! Melville! Melville!!!!"

Melville—

Age thirty-one.

Indebted.

Poor-sighted.

Landlocked.

At a table beneath a window.

Conjuring a ship full of men.

In a house full of women.

Come—no nonsense, he wrote to Hawthorne.
If you dont—I will send Constables after you.

*We will have mulled wine with wisdom, & buttered toast with story-telling
& crack jokes & bottles from morning till night.*

"Ultimately nothing counted more for him than a mate to whom he
could tell everything," according to Geoffrey O'Brien, "'mate' being a
term male and nautical rather than female and domestic."

In March, Melville once again visited the Hawthornes—
"At dusk arrived Herman Melville from Pittsfield," a very pregnant
Sophia Hawthorne recorded in her diary.

Melville had just learned that his New York house had sold for far less
than he had hoped and as a result he could not afford his mortgage
on Arrowhead, much less the multiple renovations that were already
under way.

He would need to borrow more money; *Moby-Dick* would need to be
a commercial success.

Faced with what the Biographer calls a "crushing realization," Melville escaped to the little red cottage in Lenox.

"He was entertained with Champagne foam—manufactured of
beaten eggs, loaf sugar & champagne—bread & butter & cheese,"
recorded Sophia Hawthorne.

Melville stayed the night, and the following morning he took Hawthorne and Hawthorne's seven-year-old daughter, Una, through a
snowstorm back to Arrowhead.

Una, whom Hawthorne sometimes called "Onion."

And who died in England at age thirty-three after much illness and disappointment, I've just learned.

Whose life, in Robert Hass's formulation, did not seem to work.

(Yeah, my husband said last night when I asked him if he would say his life thus far has worked.)

Before Melville left with Hawthorne and Una for Pittsfield, Sophia gave him a steel engraving of a portrait of Hawthorne.

This portrait, hanging in Melville's study at the time of his death forty years later, is now in the Herman Melville Memorial Room of the Berkshire Athenaeum, Pittsfield's public library.

The Berkshire Athenaeum will soon be the home for all of the Biographer's materials on Melville—
He has packed and mailed over seventy boxes and will send more when his health allows.

The Biographer has a long history with the Athenaeum, beginning in 1962 when he hitchhiked from New York to Pittsfield to research Melville for his dissertation.

Most days he worked in solitude until children arrived after school—
"I thought it was wonderful—little bustling students all around and Gansevoort Melville right in front of me."

The Athenaeum—just a devel of an unspellable word—is renovating its shelving to accommodate the Biographer's books, notes, and letters.

The cost of shipping and display might exceed $40,000, up to $10,000 of which the Biographer has pledged.

Jennet Cook donated $10,000 in memory of her mother, Janet, who in retirement worked as a docent at Arrowhead and conducted research for the Biographer.

One day, according to her obituary, Janet Cook was asked to return to Arrowhead after closing to give two men a private tour that ended up lasting almost three hours.

Scorsese and Tarantino—
"She had no idea who they were."

Jennet Cook "began to sob a bit" when her donation in memory of her mother was announced at a ceremony at the Athenaeum in 2019.

A local reporter covering the ceremony noted that the Athenaeum is where the Biographer "had begun his life's world."

[Sic], presumably, though suggestive.

Last year an interviewer asked the Biographer, then eighty-four, if he has completed his life's work on Melville.

"Who knows?" he said.

The Berkshire Athenaeum "is closed to public browsing and computer use effective Friday, November 13, 2020."

So no one may see the steel engraving of Hawthorne that hung on the wall of Melville's study.

So no one may see Herman Melville's 1856 passport application (height 5'8¾").

So no one may see his customs house inspector's badge (no. 75).

Or what is believed to be the desk at which he wrote *Billy Budd*.

Or the tin bread box in which Lizzie stored the manuscript after Melville's death.

Or a book, *Landseer's Dogs and Their Stories*, that Melville gave to his granddaughter Eleanor for her ninth birthday, seven months before his death.

> ELEANOR M. THOMAS
>
> FROM HER GRANDFATHER
>
> HERMAN MELVILLE
>
> FEB. 24, 1891.

For the time being the Herman Melville Memorial Room is locked and dark.

The time being thirty-two and three-quarters minutes past ten o'clock a.m. of this eleventh day of December, AD 2020.

[T]his blessed minute.

Perhaps one day I'll visit the Herman Melville Memorial Room, provided it reopens, provided I can travel.

Provided I'm still interested.

"One sheds one's sickness in books," wrote D. H. Lawrence.

"I would say that one sheds one's interest," wrote Geoff Dyer in his book about trying to write a book about Lawrence—
"One begins writing a book about something because one is interested in that subject; one finishes writing a book in order to lose interest in that subject."

But what is my subject?

All my sticky notes—
Color-coded, but I don't know the code.

Looks like your books have *bloomed*, my husband once said.

Flowers in the crannied wall, he said.

But don't look up Byron, he said.

I said, It's Tennyson.

Don't look up Tennyson, he said.
Do not google any lords.

"Melville would never have finished his book today—he'd be constantly Googling 'whale,'" according to Philip Hoare.

This orange sticky note says, "late timidity."

And this yellow one says, "Helen Vendler."

And this yellow one says, "Hawthorne himself was an inept businessman."

And this blue one is blank.

If I could pluck each one—"root and all, all in all"—they might be pages of a book called *The Endless, Winding Way*.

Or *Lucky Melville*.

Or *Under Under*.

Or *Home on the Deep*.

Or *A Long Dardenelles*.

[Sic].

Life, Melville once wrote to Sophia Hawthorne, *is a long Dardenelles*.

The shores we pass are *bright with flowers*.

We want to pluck them, he wrote, but the banks are too steep.

And so we just keep floating.

We *float on & on*, he wrote, looking for a place to land.

Until *swoop! we launch into the great sea!*

Or *The Cost of Living*, the working title of Elizabeth Hardwick's autobiographical novel, *Sleepless Nights*.

Hardwick began *Sleepless Nights* in the summer of 1973, when Robert Lowell's infamous collection *The Dolphin* was published.

In *The Dolphin*, which depicts the dissolution of their marriage, Lowell used language from Hardwick's letters, sometimes altered and without her consent—
"What does one say about a poet who, having left his wife and daughter for another marriage . . . goes on to appropriate his ex-wife's letters written under stress and pain of desertion, into a book of poems nominally addressed to the new wife?" wrote Adrienne Rich in *American Poetry Review*.

"[O]ne of the most vindictive and mean-spirited acts in the history of poetry," she called it.

Stanley Kunitz found passages to be "monstrously heartless" and "too intimately cruel."
Donald Hall called Lowell a "cannibal-poet who dines off portions of his own body, and the bodies of his family."
Elizabeth Bishop, objecting to Lowell's alteration of Hardwick's letters, famously wrote to him, "art just isn't worth that much."

Hey Siri, said my husband from the peninsula, how much is art worth?—
I don't see the stock, she replied.

The Dolphin won the Pulitzer Prize—
Gwendolyn Brooks, however, dissented from her fellow jurors, William Alfred and Anthony Hecht.

The Dolphin "hurt me as much as anything in my life," Hardwick wrote to Elizabeth Bishop.

After its publication, Lowell refused Hardwick's requests to see her letters he had used in the book, fearing she would destroy them—
He claimed he couldn't find them.

According to their daughter, Hardwick would likely have preserved the letters, given her abiding regard for archives and her principled reluctance to interfere with them.

Following Lowell's death, the letters were still kept from Hardwick—Caroline Blackwood mailed them to Frank Bidart, who kept them under his bed for ten years before giving them to the Houghton Library with instructions that they not be made available "until the death of Elizabeth Hardwick."

Hardwick died in 2007 thinking they had been lost or destroyed.

Her novel *Sleepless Nights*, published after Lowell's death, can be read as a response to *The Dolphin*.

According to Dan Chiasson, "It is not lurid, but it tells, in its way, Hardwick's own version of these years, and seems to have been written to go alongside it in a casebook of the controversy."

Hardwick said the book grew out of a single line: "Now I will start my novel, but I don't know whether to call myself I or she."

She chose "I."
> E.g.: "I am alone here in New York, no longer a *we*."
> "Here I am with my hibiscus blooming in the bay window."
> "Can it be that I am the subject?"

Her story, she wrote, "certainly hasn't the drama of: I saw the old, white-bearded frigate master on the dock and signed up for the journey"—
"But after all, 'I' am a woman."

[sic passim]

Hardwick wrote *Sleepless Nights* over a period of years.

"I am simply terrified of writing on this soi-disant novel," she wrote to Lowell in January 1976.
"It goes about one trembling paragraph per day; confidence drips away painfully and one can't imagine it even being printed much less read."

In *Sleepless Nights*, she faced the problem of how to write about Lowell, their twenty-three years of marriage—
Her solution—"a brilliant technical stroke," according to Mary McCarthy—was not to.

Lowell, McCarthy wrote to Hardwick, "becomes a sort of black hole in outer space, to be filled in ad lib, which is poetic justice: he's condemned by the *form* to non-existence—you couldn't do that in a conventional autobiography."

Sleepless Nights follows no plot, owes no influences, belongs to no genre.

"[O]ne of the most original books I have read," according to Sigrid Nunez.

"[A] feat of originality," according to Lauren Groff, who keeps four extra copies "just in case someone comes over for a party or dinner or something, and I can just press it into their hands."

She finds the book explosive yet comforting, both "bomb" and "balm."

It's the book Groff has read most frequently during her own sleepless nights.

One of the first times she read it (aloud, quietly) was while nursing her son—
"This is a book that's so beautiful that I would just continue reading with him sleeping in my arms in the middle of the night."

The book I most remember reading with an infant in my arms in the middle of the night is *Howards End*.

An old paperback, bright green.

Borrowed without permission years earlier from my father's house, and still unreturned.

A Vintage edition with a striking cover—three abstract tree trunks, two white, one black, curving to an emerald cloud of leaves.

Fair condition, cover creased, corners worn, spine sunned, pages foxed.

No marks, no dog-ears, no easy way to find the lethal shower of books.

"Nothing had sense" (page 324).

The bookmark in Chapter XXII is my boarding pass for Delta 1483, Atlanta to Miami, seat 41A, 10 March 2002.

I was thirty-one.

Incidentally, Forster's age when he published *Howards End*.
("My best novel," he called it nearly fifty years later, "and approaching a good novel.")

In four months I'd be married, in three years rereading *Howards End* in a nursery in the middle of the night.

Now I'm fifty, as of yesterday.

Issa, at fifty:

> From now on,
>   it's all clear profit,
>   every sky.

It's not that it's *old*, my daughter said, it just seems like a long time. Like, a lot happens.

It just so happens.

A bottle of Heidsieck, a great white cake—
I made my dull and vital wish.

("Living is not an original business," according to Yiyun Li.)

This morning is the morning after—
Clear profit, every sky.

In the fall of 1964 Elizabeth Bishop, then age fifty-three, wrote to Robert Lowell that she currently knew three poets who were "busy commenting" about the anguish of turning fifty.

"I did attempt something about being forty-five once, and my eyebrows getting rather bald," she wrote to Lowell, "but it didn't turn out well and thank heavens I've never wanted to try the subject of one's years again."

"When we blow out our birthday candles each year, our eyebrows age with us, too," according to *Self* magazine.

Five known species undergo menopause, I've recently learned, and four of them are whales: beluga, killer, short-finned pilot, and narwhal.

Studies of whale pods show that the presence of post-reproductive females increases survival rates of young whales—
The so-called "grandmother effect," I told my husband.

I told him that postmenopausal whales often lead their pods on the hunt for food.

So for whales, I said, menopause is actually an adaptive trait.

"This was an idea that I really, really liked," said Darcey Steinke, who became obsessed with whales while writing *Flash Count Diary*, her book on menopause.

She read about them, watched them on YouTube, listened for them on a live-linked hydrophone—
When sad, she'd "double down," watching recorded whales while listening for live ones.

During one of Steinke's sleepless nights her husband said to her, "You know when you go away from the whales, it seems like you don't do so well, but when you stay with the whales, it seems like you do really well."

Steinke traveled to Sea World "to be near a postmenopausal whale"—Lolita, a killer whale who has been in captivity for fifty years—and to join a protest for her release.

She traveled to San Juan Island to see the pod from which Lolita was captured in 1970.

On her first day on the Salish Sea, Steinke and her group saw a pod rapidly approaching their kayaks—
She felt herself to be, she writes in *Flash Count Diary*, "a small land creature floating on the edge of a vast ocean populated by giants."

She watched the massive whales swim beneath their boats, and came eye-to-eye with the iconic elder, Granny, aka J2—the whale she had most hoped to see.

"I'm still not really over it," she said in an interview.
"I'll never get over it."

For Steinke, who loves *Moby-Dick*, it was difficult not to see herself as a version of Ishmael and her book a feminist version of Melville's—
"I got obsessed with that whale, I got into that boat, I chased that whale."

"I did that."

While camping during her second trip west to view whales, she spent a terrifying, rainy night alone in her tent on Stuart Island.

In the fading natural light she struggled to read the small print in her copy of *Moby-Dick*.

Later, having woken in profound dark to the sound of rustling, she swung the book against the side of the tent to ward off whatever lurked outside.

Having overslept before departing for the island, Steinke had forgotten her cell phone, flashlight, headlamp, warm jacket, and knit cap—but she remembered *Moby-Dick*.

A novel that Melville believed would not be of interest to women.

Two months before its publication, he wrote to his friend and neighbor Sarah Morewood, *It is not a peice of fine feminine Spitalfields silk—but is of the horrible texture of a fabric that should be woven of ships' cables & hausers.*

Dont you buy it—dont you read it.

Later, when Sophia Hawthorne wrote to commend him on the book, he responded with surprise—
It is true that some _men_ have said they were pleased with it, but you are the only _woman_—
for as a general thing, women have small taste for the sea.

"The first three times I tried *Moby-Dick*, I gave it up with disgust," said Lauren Groff, "and the fourth time, it changed my life."

After several failed attempts to get through the novel ("It seemed overblown, and too full of men"), Margaret Drabble finally "completed the voyage" in 1999, and now considers *Moby-Dick* one of the greatest novels in the English language.

"How could I have missed, on my first attempts, the extraordinary human diversity that this novel portrays?" she asks.

"Every time I read it I feel as if my mind is larger," said Marilynne Robinson, who has taught the book repeatedly and, according to one of her former students, has "yet to shed her astonishment."

While rereading *Moby-Dick*, Sylvia Plath wrote in her journal, "am whelmed and wondrous at the swimming Biblical & craggy Shakespearean cadences, the rich & lustrous & fragrant recreation of spermaceti, ambergris—miracle, marvel, the ton-thunderous leviathan."

This quote fits, just barely, on a yellow sticky note.
It might serve as scrip—
might cover, just barely, the cost of rousing my husband in some dark hour.

I'd tell him that Plath wrote that one of her "few wishes" was to be "aboard a whale ship through the process of turning a monster to light & heat."

At this time she was twenty-five, and had a life expectancy of about sixty-three.

I had forgotten, until my husband reminded me while we were making dinner, that years ago when we saw the Sylvia Plath biopic the film reel broke with about ten minutes remaining.

The lights came on, eventually an employee addressed the scant crowd: the reel, he explained, could not be repaired and, since this happened to be the movie's final showing at that theater, it could not be replaced.

We received free passes to some other movie, and we walked out into the snow.

Behind us we heard an elderly couple lamenting that now they'd never know how it ended.

As it turns out, the years have not made clearer whether we should have told them.

Maybe her husband would leave his lover and come back to her.
Maybe they'd return to Devon with the children in time for spring.
Maybe the poems she was writing would be celebrated.
Maybe she would sleep and be well again.

When the Biographer set out to tell the life of Herman Melville he knew too well how it would end.

accidents
aging, effects of
death, attitude toward
debts
defaults on loans
destroys letters
employment as customs inspector
gossip, subject of
illnesses and health
invisibility
marriage
poverty, attitude toward
reclusiveness
sanity questioned

The Biographer's solution was to write the second half of his biography first—
"I was afraid if I waited until I had written the first half I would not be strong enough to tell such a sad story."

Drafting Volume 2 was, he wrote, "the hardest intellectual, emotional, and aesthetic feat I ever accomplished."

Another legendary Melvillean, Henry A. Murray, never found a way to write about the second half of Melville's life.

Murray worked intermittently on a biography of Melville for over twenty years, but could not get past 1852, when Melville completed *Pierre*, the novel that destroyed his literary career.

According to one reviewer, *Pierre* "might be supposed to emanate from a lunatic hospital rather than from the quiet retreats of Berkshire."

"HERMAN MELVILLE CRAZY," declared one newspaper headline.

Melville wrote *Pierre*, which was published less than ten months after *Moby-Dick*, at his usual frenzied and injurious pace—
Friends and family members, including one prominent physician, worried about his health and sanity.

"To read *Pierre*," writes one biographer, "is to feel the discomfort one feels in the presence of a brilliant friend who, in the grip of some new passion, has gone 'over the top.'"

Another biographer claims that it reads "like a narrative nervous breakdown."

Last night the low was four degrees, and my husband asked what *Pierre* was about.

We were wide awake in the dark, like some pre-industrial couple between their first and second sleeps.

Pierre Glendinning, I told him, is an heir to a country estate. His father died when he was young, like Melville's. He's close to his mom in kind of a creepy way. She wants him to marry a dull, good socialite—kind of like Lizzie, I said. But a mysterious young woman shows up, claiming to be his illegitimate half sister. She lives in a little red farmhouse covered with moss. (Hawthorne alert, my husband said.) Pierre decides to break off his engagement with Lucy, the socialite, and fake-marry the mystery woman, Isabel. I think to take care of her without exposing the family secret? His mother freaks out, as does Pierre, who renounces his claim to the estate and takes off for New York City with Isabel. (How much more? my husband said.) They probably commit incest, I told him. Pierre also seems to have had a possibly incestuous relationship with his cousin Glen. Glen lives in

New York, and when Pierre reaches out, he rejects his request for help. Pierre is all of a sudden a writer. (Melville got angry at the terms of his publishing contract, I explained, and seems to have added the writer plot to disparage the literary culture and industry.) He writes all day in a cold room, he doesn't eat, he doesn't sleep, he can't write the book he wants to write. Isabel copies his pages and plays her weird guitar. (What guitar? my husband asked.) Pierre's mother dies and he learns that Glen is the heir to the estate. Also he's trying to marry Lucy. Lucy, though, is still in love with Pierre and flees to New York, where she lives with Pierre and Isabel. Pierre, I said, pretends that Lucy is his cousin. (So he's pretending that his sister is his wife, my husband said, and that his fiancée is his cousin. Right, I said. He also calls his mother "sister" and she calls him "brother.") When Pierre turns in his book to his publisher, the publisher gets mad because Pierre promised a popular book and delivered something else. Glen comes to the city to try to rescue Lucy. I think someone else is with him, I said, and Pierre shoots them. He goes to jail. When Isabel and Lucy visit him, Lucy dies of shock. Pierre and Isabel then drink poison and perish.

But where, my husband wanted to know, was the ocean.

"[A]t sea on land," Updike calls Melville, I see this morning.

"The third of the world that is dry land and the half that is the female sex turned the compass of his imagination away," he writes.

Updike argues that in *Moby-Dick* Melville spent the remainder of his "artistic capital, his years at sea"—
Never in literary history, he speculates, has anyone written such a good book followed by such a bad book.

So, now, let us add Moby Dick to our blessing, and step from that, Melville wrote to Hawthorne just after its publication—

Then, presumably speaking of his ambition for *Pierre*, already under way: *Leviathan is not the biggest fish;—I have heard of Krakens.*

According to Jill Lepore, Melville viewed these books "as twins, each penetrating psychological depths"—
Deep, deep, and still deep and deeper must we go, Melville wrote in *Pierre*, *if we would find out the heart of a man; descending into which is as descending a spiral stair in a shaft, without any end, and where that endlessness is only concealed by the spiralness of the stair, and the blackness of the shaft.*

Melville was "the greatest depth psychologist America ever produced," according to Henry A. Murray, would-be Melville biographer and onetime director of the Harvard Psychological Clinic—
A "Columbus of the mind," Murray called him.

In his renowned ninety-page introduction to *Pierre*, he claims that Melville is "the literary discoverer" of the unconscious.

Murray hoped that writing this introduction would help him complete the biography of Melville that he had begun more than twenty years earlier.

His first encounter with Melville was aboard a ship crossing the Atlantic in 1924 when he was thirty-one—
A friend had given him a copy of *Moby-Dick*, calling it "a good sea yarn by an unknown author."

Upon beginning the novel, Murray immediately felt, he later said, a "shock of recognition"—
an allusion to Melville's encounter with Hawthorne's *Mosses from an Old Manse* (also at age thirty-one).

"I was swept by Melville's gale and shaken by his appalling sea dragon," wrote Murray, who began to be visited by Melville in dreams.

Profoundly inspired by what he called Melville's "wandering in the deep," Murray, who was trained as a medical doctor, decided to become a psychologist.

Get this, my husband told me, Murray, while on board the *Scythia*, assisted a British doctor who performed an emergency appendectomy on the ship's captain, and that British doctor turned out to be a Melville fanatic who had crossed the Atlantic just to spend four days in New Bedford learning more about Melville, and after they saved the captain's life they went to the lounge for drinks and ended up talking about this obscure American writer.

He also told me that Murray's first hero was Norwegian explorer Fridtjof Nansen—
As a boy of not yet four, Murray once refused to go to bed until his parents agreed to name his infant brother Nansen.

They named him Cecil, my husband said.

Last week he had a long wait for his physical therapy appointment and the only book in our car was my ILL copy of *Love's Story Told: A Life of Henry A. Murray*, which he has now nearly completed.

Not because he finds it compelling—This guy's life makes me so tired, he said—but because he's compelled to finish any book he starts.

While I was making dinner last night (Asian bowls), he told me about Murray's obsessive research of Melville's life.

Murray climbed Mount Greylock, corresponded with Julian Haw-

thorne, tracked down and purchased letters, courted Melville's
relatives—

He even gave an Airedale puppy to the granddaughters of Melville's
brother.

He tried to buy Arrowhead, my husband told me.

On Murray's first visit to Melville's farm he began to quake—

He let himself into the house, "mounted to old Vulcan's workroom,
opened the shutters and stood there in tremulous, holy awe."

He sat at Melville's desk, slept in Melville's bed.

On some visit he tore boards off the barn at Arrowhead and installed
them on the wall of his own study.

Murray spent the next twenty years working on his biography of
Melville as time allowed.

After ten years, he hadn't yet reached Melville's first book—

"I have written about 400 typewritten pages," he wrote to a friend,
"but have only got Herman as far as Tahiti."

After ten more years, he had over a thousand pages extending through
the publication of *Pierre*.

During this time, a period known as the "Melville Revival," Murray
exasperated scholars by failing to publish or share the information he
had obtained from Melville's relatives.

In 1947 one prominent Melvillean expressed his frustration that a
generation of scholars had "stewed around in ignorance" due to Murray's withholding—

"It just makes me think what a general fuck-up the whole Melville business has been."

In an unpublished interview shortly before his death, Murray allegedly confirmed what many had long suspected: that he held secrets related to Melville.

He indicated that before his death he would divulge this information—which many believe pertained to violence within the Melville household—but if he did, that information has not been made public.

Murray's massive unfinished biography is part of the thirty-one boxes of his Melville materials in the collection at Harvard Library.

"Now, there are two kinds of biographers," according to the Biographer, "the great accumulators and the doers."

When you die with a secret, he wrote, "someone comes along and realizes that you were not smart enough, did not know enough, did not have imagination enough, to make sense of the great document you had been clutching to your bosom for decades."

After Murray's death, the Biographer "diplomatically suggested" to his widow that she tear into the wall of his study behind the boards taken from Arrowhead.

In that wall there may be a safe, and in that safe there may be letters, and among those letters, the Biographer believes, may be ones Melville wrote to Hawthorne—
Murray's widow, however, "declined to wreck a perfectly good wall."

Marriage was Melville's wall, according to Murray, his prison—

just as the whale was Ahab's wall, and Wall Street was Bartleby's wall.

By Murray's count, Melville committed "seventeen egressions" before his marriage to Lizzie, at which point, given the conventions of the time, escape was no longer an option.

It has been suggested that Murray was incapable of completing his biography of Melville because he knew too much about, and identified too strongly with, Melville's troubled marriage.

Like Melville, Murray married a wealthy, good-natured, well-bred woman from Boston—
Josephine Rantoul, whose childhood home, I see on Google Maps, is a mile from the childhood home of Elizabeth Shaw.

Throughout most of this marriage, Murray was involved in a relationship with Christiana Morgan, another Boston Brahmin, also married, who served as a muse to Carl Jung and subsequently collaborated with Murray at the Harvard Psychological Clinic.

Jung, who used Morgan's trance-induced drawings of images from her unconscious as the basis of his Visions Seminars, referred to her as his "Olympus," and regarded her as a *femme inspiratrice*.

"Your function is to create a man," he told her—
"If you create Murray you will have done something very fine for the world."

Morgan and Murray together created the Thematic Apperception Test, still used today, which requires subjects to develop narratives based on a series of ambiguous pictures.

They considered their greatest creation, however, their relationship itself, which was inspired by Melville and in particular *Pierre*.

In Pierre and Isabel's relationship, governed, as Murray and Morgan saw it, by the unconscious rather than conventional morality, they recognized their own—
incest and suicide notwithstanding.

According to Murray's biographer, Murray and Morgan believed their union would "show the way to others and thus earn canonization for their love."

Together they planned to write a book, a "trance epic"—
"I do not know of anything as big as this ever being attempted, but I feel fully capable of doing it *with you*," Murray wrote to Morgan.

(Avoid adjectives of scale, cautioned Bashō.)

This project, variously conceived over decades, was never completed.

Murray's energy and attention were continually diverted by psychology and Melville, a source of frustration to Morgan—
"Lover," she once wrote to him, "you must choose between me and Melville."

The Melville Ultimatum, my husband said.

Morgan's section of what they referred to as "The Book," or "our Book," or the *Proposition*, came to be called *What Joy!* while Murray's was called *Challenge*.

Whereas Morgan produced several hundred pages, Murray made little progress—

The *Proposition* was one of eleven books that he left unfinished.

One project they did complete was their Tower on the Parker River in Massachusetts.

Did I know about the Tower, my husband asked me last night when I was certain he was asleep.

Some sort of monument to the relationship, he said, with three stories representing mind, body, and spirit.

Decorated with symbolic artwork—carvings, quotations, paintings, sculptures, stained glass.

Some surprising stuff happening on the second floor, he said.

Whips, chains, a knife.

He turned on his light and read me one of Murray's decrees to Morgan: "Thou shalt be my slave until I have finished Melville to your utter satisfaction."

Then he turned his light off.

Melville planned to build a tower, I told him.

And Hawthorne built a tower in Concord that he called his "sky-parlor."

Jung had a tower on a lake, he told me.

Yeats had a tower on a river, I told him.

His wife would fish from the window.

I told him about her voluminous automatic writing, supposedly guided by spirits, which fascinated Yeats and supplied him with material.

There's a biography of her I'd like to read, I told him, but it's eight hundred pages.

I told him that James Merrill's partner, a failed novelist, used a Ouija board to generate the material for Merrill's three-volume epic poem *The Changing Light at Sandover*.

Merrill once said in an interview, I said, that the poem should perhaps have been published under both of their names.

But did they have a tower? my husband asked.

Yes, I said, they did.

My husband asked me if I knew Robinson Jeffers, and I said I did.

Robinson Jeffers had a tower in California, he said.

Do you need a tower to finish Melville to my satisfaction? he asked.

I said nobody ever finishes Melville to anyone's satisfaction, and that's when he said bon voyage.

This morning I watched *The Tower*, a twenty-six-minute documentary made by Christiana Morgan's granddaughter.

Morgan, I learned, helped clear the land for construction—

"cutting down trees, pulling brush for the burning, tearing out the stumps, hauling wood, digging the earth," she recorded in her diary.

In the evening, after an exhausting day of work, she would walk out "to see the new shape of the things that [her] labor had brought about."

She hired a local carpenter named Kenneth Knight, who used dynamite to create the foundation for the Tower—
His son, David, age eighty-six in the documentary, recalls watching rocks fly through the air.

Knight, who brought materials in by wheelbarrow, built the Tower by hand in a year and a half.

"He was a master, it always came out perfect," his son said, or says—
"He would never, ever compromise his work."

Knight taught Morgan how to use his wood-carving tools, with which she created intricate artwork that celebrated her union with Murray.

She also made paintings, planted gardens, and commissioned stained-glass and iron works based on her visions and iconography—
"The chief feature of this whole place," she wrote in the prologue to *What Joy!*, "is that everything—pretty nearly everything, inside and outside—is symbolic."

In the Tower, Morgan and Murray engaged in elaborate ceremonies and rituals—
erotic, culinary, intellectual, spiritual.

(Morgan's granddaughter recalls that if Murray's black car was in the driveway she was not to enter the Tower.)

"You see, the Tower isn't just a house," Morgan wrote to her son, "it represents a way of life—Harry's and my life for forty years."
"It has been for both of us as if we are writing a book—it is there for anyone who has the eyes to see or to comprehend."

"Now, if you were writing a book, which took you forty years," she wrote, "wouldn't you like to know that it was going out into the wider world?"

Murray, for his part, told his biographer that even if they hadn't written anything about their relationship, it would be expressed and memorialized by the Tower.

Near the end of her life, Morgan changed her will, stipulating that upon the death of her son the property would pass to a neighboring private school, which she believed would maintain it in perpetuity.

But in a symposium session I watched online this morning I learned that the school has used the Tower for faculty housing and that it has fallen into disrepair—
The roof has leaked, the stained glass has cracked and bowed, the gardens have disappeared.

A recent photo shows air-conditioning units in the ornate windows.

According to a 2017 article in the school newspaper, residents of Morgan Tower—"located just off the cross country trail"—have, through the years, seen Morgan's ghost or sensed her presence.

Morgan died in 1967 at the age of sixty-nine while on vacation with Murray in the Virgin Islands—
perhaps an inebriated accident but almost certainly a suicide.

She had hoped the trip would rejuvenate their relationship, but Murray, who had become involved with a woman more than twenty years younger than Morgan, was distracted and inattentive.

On the morning of March 14 Morgan drowned in the shallow lagoon below their cottage.

"You disgust me!" Murray had said to her as she woke hungover in bed; or, "You're disgusting," he had said to her as she drank on the beach that morning.

Depending on the biography.

It's impossible to say what happened next because Murray, in a series of distraught letters to friends, presented numerous and conflicting accounts of the morning's events—
"Christiana was robbed even in death," according to her biographer, "this time by the muffled reports of her tragic statement."

The circumstances of Murray's death, incidentally, were far less ambiguous—
He died of pneumonia twenty-one years later at the age of ninety-five.

"I am dead," he told his nurse days before his death.
When she disagreed, pinching him gently on his cheek, he said, "I'm the doctor; you're the nurse, and I'm dead."

Last night I asked my husband if Murray's biography mentions that Morgan took off the emerald ring he had given her thirty years earlier, wrapped it in her beach bag, and placed it on the sand before walking into the lagoon.

He said no and asked if Morgan's biography mentions that Murray had drifted off to sleep on the beach that morning because he had not yet recovered from a tooth extraction.

I said no and asked if Murray's biography mentions that Morgan had that morning left a book open to a poem by Conrad Aiken with a stanza marked "To be read over my grave."

He said no and asked if Morgan's biography mentions that Murray, waking from his nap, spotted Morgan facedown in the water, dragged her body to shore, and tried to resuscitate her for over an hour.

No, I said.

What was that stanza from Aiken? he asked.

I said the book was in the other room.

The house was cold—
Both of us waited to see who would go get it.

W hat pertains?

What ought to be retrieved, even in the cold dark?

Among all Melville biographers, only the Biographer mentions the Naushon Island guest register that Melville signed on July 13, 1852.

He was touring the Massachusetts coast with his father-in-law just before the calamitous reviews of *Pierre* began to appear.

("The amount of utter trash in the volume is almost infinite.")

Sweet shall be the memory of Naushon, Melville wrote in the register.

> *Blue sky—blue sea—& almost every thing blue*
> *but our spirits.*

According to the Biographer, Melville, who lived nearly forty more years, would never be happy again.

"Got thru July 1852," he recorded in the diary he kept while writing his biography—
"Saddest line in bk," he wrote of his own claim that the trip to Naushon Island was Melville's final happy day.

The next day he wrote, "Every thing blue but our spirits—the last day when he could even pretend to be happy—A profoundly disturbing effect on me—But pushing."

And the next: "Heavy emotions because of realization about HM's never being happy again."

The disastrous *Pierre*, the catastrophic *Pierre*, the ruinous *Pierre*.

After *Pierre*, according to Geoffrey O'Brien, Melville "would never let himself go like that again"—
He suffered "a separation from language as he had loved it, primordial and generous."

One of the first pieces Melville published after *Pierre* was "Bartleby, the Scrivener," serialized anonymously in *Putnam's* magazine in late 1853.

Only sixteen months separate the "hysterical burlesque" of *Pierre* from the "austere minimalism" of "Bartleby," in the words of Elizabeth Hardwick.

Melville, erstwhile citizen of what James Wood called a "city of words," imprisoned Bartleby in a cramped linguistic cell.

I count, this morning, just two hundred and forty-three words of speech directly attributed to Bartleby, and just seventy-eight words in his lexicon:

I | would | prefer | not | to | what | is | wanted | at | present | give | no | answer | be | a | little | reasonable | left | alone | here | more | do | you | see | the | reason | for | yourself | have | given | up | copying | quit | sitting | upon | banister | make | any | change | there | too | much | confinement | about | that | like | clerkship | but | am | particular | take | it | all | though | as | said | before | doing | something | else | does | strike | me | thing | definite | stationary | know | and | want | nothing | say | where | dine | today | disagree | with | unused | dinners

The limits of Bartleby's language create, according to Hardwick, "an expressiveness literally limitless."

At present I would prefer not to be a little reasonable—
"Radical as Ahab," my husband wrote, circa 1991, in the parsimonious margin of his Dover Thrift Edition of *Bartleby and Benito Cereno*.

That's my writing but it's definitely not my thinking, he told me when I showed it to him.

He told me that his Self and Society professor, Dr. Owens, would read "Bartleby" aloud on Fridays.

Dr. Owens walked with a cane, my husband told me, and smoked through class.

He'd read a page, then stop and say, "What's here for us?"

I liked it, my husband said.

Did you participate? I asked.

Yes, but I didn't talk, he said.

"Bartleby, the Scrivener" was written for money and published anonymously, as was "Benito Cereno" in 1855.

"The Encantadas," also published at this time, appeared under the name Salvator R. Tarnmoor.

These and Melville's numerous other magazine stories of this period, though "slightly *chastened*" in style, nevertheless represent for John Updike "a triumphant recovery from the hectic tropes of *Pierre*."

But between *Pierre* and the magazine work there is a missing book, written with characteristic speed, rejected by his publisher, and subsequently lost or destroyed.

From the peninsula my husband nodded as if he'd long suspected a missing manuscript.

The lost book, called *The Isle of the Cross*, was inspired by a reputedly true story Melville was told while traveling with his father-in-law in the summer of 1852.

The story was about a young woman on the New England coast named Agatha Hatch, who cared for and married a shipwrecked sailor, only to be abandoned with a daughter for seventeen years, during which time she remained steadfast and faithful.

The tale captivated Melville, perhaps, according to the Biographer, because Melville "may have been seeing himself in a new role of passive acceptor of his fate."

Or perhaps, I see this morning, because of some other reason.

Melville was convinced that the story of Agatha could form the basis of a novel, though he was equally convinced that not he but Hawthorne should write it.

To be plump, Melville wrote to Hawthorne in the six-page "Agatha Letter," *I think that in this matter you would make a better hand at it than I would.*

To that end, Melville, as *Steward*, presented Hawthorne not only with source material but also, having *a little turned the subject over in [his] mind*, some suggestions for writing the book.

> That *Supposing the story to open with the wreck—then there must be a storm.*
> That but it should begin with the *faint shadow of the preceding* <u>*calm*</u>.
> That the setting is a sheep pasture on a high cliff above the sea.
> That *The afternoon is mild & warm.*
> That *The sea with an air of solemn deliberation, with an elaborate deliberation, ceremoniously rolls upon the beach.*
> That *The air is suppressedly charged with the sound of long lines of surf.*
> That Agatha then comes walking along the cliff.
> (That *but you must give her some other name.*)
> That Agatha *reclines along the edge of the cliff & gazes out seaward.*
> That she sees distant clouds and, as she is of a *maratime family,* she knows a storm is coming.
> That from the cliff she can see the shadow of the cliff far below on the sand.
> That, looking down at the shadow of the cliff, she then sees *a shadow moving along the shadow.*
> That the moving shadow is made by a sheep.
> That the sheep *has advanced to the very edge of the cliff, & is sending a mild innocent glance far out upon the water.*
> That *There, in strange & beautiful contrast, we have the innocence of the land placidly eyeing the malignity of the sea.*

In one of several addenda, Melville tells Hawthorne that once

Agatha's husband has been absent for some time *we must introduce the mail-post*:

> That it is a *little rude wood box with a lid to it & a leather hinge*.
> That for seventeen years Agatha *goes thither daily*.
> That *As her hopes gradually decay in her, so does the post itself & the little box decay*.
> That *grass grows rankly about it*.
> That *At last a little bird nests in it*.
> That *At last the post falls*.

This was not the first time that someone had tried, unsuccessfully, to persuade Hawthorne to write a novel about a virtuous and long-suffering woman—
Years earlier, the Reverend Horace Conolly repeatedly tried to convince him to take up the legend of a young Acadian woman who became separated from her lover, spent most of her life waiting and searching for him, then found him in old age as he was dying in a hospital.

"It is not in my vein," Hawthorne would reply, according to Conolly.

One night, at a dinner with Longfellow, Conolly again urged Hawthorne to write this story, and Hawthorne again demurred—
"It is not in my vein; there are no strong lights and heavy shadows."

"What is the story?" Longfellow asked.
"Do tell it; perhaps it will be in my vein."

Over the course of an hour, Conolly then told the story—better than he ever had, in Hawthorne's estimation.

Longfellow declared it "the best illustration of faithfulness and the constancy of woman that I have ever heard of or read," and asked Hawthorne if he could use the material for a poem.

Hawthorne consented, but on the way home he erupted in anger at Conolly for telling the story so engagingly—
"I don't think the annals of profanity could furnish a parallel to his tirade of wrath on this occasion," Conolly recalled.

"Hawthorne, if great in nothing else, was transcendently great in profanity and swearing," wrote Conolly.

Inspired by Conolly's story, Longfellow eventually wrote his epic poem *Evangeline*, which went through six printings in six months, and sold thirty-six thousand copies in its first ten years.

(Hawthorne, I see, published a rave review of *Evangeline* in the Salem *Advertiser*.)

Between the publication of *Evangeline* and his receipt of Melville's "Agatha Letter," Hawthorne published his own tale of the preternaturally resolute heroine—
Hester Prynne, a woman of "fanatical stamina," according to Elizabeth Hardwick.

Betrayed heroines such as Hester have "a sense of reality, a curious sort of independence and honor, an acceptance of consequence that puts courage to the most searing test."

Hester's qualities are, according to Hardwick, a "cause for wonder."

Analogously, the qualities Hardwick demonstrated during her tumultuous years with Lowell have been regarded as a cause for wonder.

"She must have been one of the sanest and most generous women who ever lived," Helen Vendler writes in a review of the late correspondence collected in *The Dolphin Letters*.

"There is scarcely a virtue that Hardwick is not seen to exemplify in these years."

"Hardwick on the whole maintains a superhuman composure and decency," writes another reviewer of the *The Dolphin Letters*.

Multiple reviewers refer to her as the heroine of this collection— "She fits the description she herself gives in 'Seduction and Betrayal' of 'the betrayed heroine,'" according to one recent piece.

When Lowell's marriage to Blackwood became untenable, Hardwick took him back—albeit more as a friend than a spouse.

To Mary McCarthy she wrote that she was "not at all as vulnerable" to Lowell as she once was—
"We are trying to work out a sort of survival for both of us, and both are sixty."

After spending the summer of 1977 with Hardwick in Maine, Lowell flew to Ireland to see Blackwood and their son but returned earlier than scheduled because he was restless and unhappy.

He died of a heart attack in the taxi that was bringing him from the airport to Hardwick's apartment—
When Hardwick met the taxi, she found Lowell unresponsive, holding a portrait of Caroline Blackwood painted by Blackwood's former husband Lucian Freud.

I think he planned to get it appraised, I told my husband.

I also told him that after Lowell was pronounced dead at the hospital, Hardwick paid someone ten dollars for a dime to call her daughter.

The following spring Hardwick returned to the house in Maine, where Lowell's "red shirt and socks were a painful discovery."

"The death is unacceptable," she wrote to Elizabeth Bishop, "and yet I know he has gone."

Lowell's briefcase remained in Hardwick's study for years after he died—
"Cigarettes, cigarette lighter, nail file, glasses still there," she wrote to McCarthy around 1980.

Among other items in the briefcase was a red 1973 desk diary, eight-by-six inches, which Lowell was still using at the time of his death in 1977.

Some pages include personal notes and reminders in Lowell's "near-illegible handwriting," but many contain fragments and drafts of poems, revised versions of which appeared in *Day by Day*, Lowell's final collection.

Weeks before his death Lowell inscribed a copy of *Day by Day* for Hardwick:

FOR LIZZIE,

WHO SNATCHED ME OUT OF

CHAOS,

WITH ALL MY LOVE

IN CASTINE AUG. 1977

CAL

This morning, having retrieved my collected Lowell, I discover that my husband gave it to me in 2004 on our second wedding anniversary.

He inscribed it with a quotation from a poem that—I see now—appeared in *Day by Day*:

> Bright sun of my bright day,
> I thank God for being alive—

He had a younger man's handwriting.

He has, I've just learned, no recollection of giving me the book, much less inscribing it.

As I have no recollection of receiving it.

Perhaps someday we'll discover what I gave him that day.
A Saturday, I see.

"[T]he battered calendar of the past, the back-glancing flow of numbers," Hardwick wrote near the end of *Sleepless Nights*.

"The old pages of the days and weeks are splattered with the dark-brown rings of coffee cups and I find myself gratefully dissolved in the grounds as the water drips downward."

> Gratefully dissolved
> in the grounds as the water
> drips downward on days

"Oh, the dear grave," Hardwick said to an interviewer at age sixty-eight—
"I like what Gottfried Benn wrote, something like, 'May I die in the spring when the ground is soft and easy to plough.'"

"Christ, / may I die at night," begins the final stanza of an unfinished poem Robert Lowell was working on in the days before his death.

I have now no serious, no insuperable objections to a respectable longevity,
Melville wrote to his brother-in-law at age forty-three, his arm in a
sling following a serious carriage accident—
I dont like the idea of being left out night after night in a cold church-yard.

Melville was buried in Woodlawn Cemetery in the Bronx next to his
two sons.

On his tombstone there is an unfurled scroll, a common motif of the
period—
But Melville's scroll is blank, a rare variation.

"Speculation abounds," I see.

T he Melville Medal, invented by John Updike in his novel *Bech Is Back*, is given every five years to the American author "who has maintained the most meaningful silence."

Melville's late silence was for decades a matter of consensus.

The first biography, by Raymond Weaver in 1921, established the long-standing view of Melville as someone who was finished as a writer by the midpoint of his life—
Weaver devotes just two of seventeen chapters to his life after *Moby-Dick*, and calls his final novel, *The Confidence-Man*, published in 1857 when Melville was thirty-seven, "a posthumous work."

Melville's career, according to Weaver, "is like a star that drops a line of streaming fire down the vault of the sky—and then the dark and blasted shape that sinks into the earth."

Recent biographies, however, pay more attention to the poetry Melville wrote after his twelve-year career as a prose writer—
His *Complete Poems* runs to nearly a thousand pages.

Almost all of Melville's poetry was written after he and his family moved in 1863 from Arrowhead to his final residence at 104 East Twenty-Sixth Street in New York.

The house in which the Melvilles lived no longer stands and street numbers have shifted through the years, but tax records and atlases allowed Melville scholars to determine its exact location.

(A municipal listing from 1882: "Owner, Elizabeth S. Melville; Size of Lot, 20 x 98; Size of House, 20 x 45; Stories, 3; Value of Real Estate, $6,500.")

On a cold winter afternoon in 1981, about forty members of the Melville Society, several of whom wore ties with spouting whales, gathered to install a bronze plaque commemorating the spot.

Located just outside of a delivery entrance to a seven-story office building at 357 Park Avenue South, the plaque reads:

HERMAN MELVILLE

THE AMERICAN AUTHOR

RESIDED FROM 1863–1891 AT THIS SITE

104 EAST 26TH STREET

WHERE HE WROTE

BILLY BUDD

AMONG OTHER WORKS

This plaque cost $173, according to the Melville Society newsletter, and "was guided through production by Mr. Charles Neumeier of Stuyvesant High School, our man in New York who also made all of the physical arrangements for the gathering."

This morning I see that in 1976 Neumeier and a colleague at Stuyvesant organized a fundraiser for restorations of Arrowhead—
Their students ("budding Melvilleans") raised $200 by hosting a festival, a bike tour, and excursions to see the play *Benito Cereno*, written by Robert Lowell.

"The lessons Mr. Neumeier taught me have lasted a lifetime," one of his former students wrote on an AIDS memorial site at Columbia University, where Neumeier received an MA.

He was, his former student wrote, "a quiet and very unassuming man" with a "soft voice."

Although, as this student notes, it was challenging to be a gay teacher at Stuyvesant at that time, Neumeier "never showed us his struggles"—Instead, he consistently demonstrated the "love and joy he had for our wonderful language."

A paywall blocks the full-sized image, but if I squint I can see him in the thumbnail image of a page from the 1976 Stuyvesant High School yearbook—
at the blackboard, candid.

I can also see, on the adjacent page, his colleague Frank McCourt, who also, it turns out, taught *Moby-Dick* to Stuyvesant students.

"I mean, the whale was in our classroom," said one of McCourt's former students after his death in 2009.

Neumeier died in 1985 at age fifty-four in Key West—
three and a half years after he organized the plaque ceremony, which the Melville Society newsletter describes as "a joyous occasion."

Among the members present was the Biographer, although he was not yet, I suppose, the Biographer.

He began writing his biography eight years later on the afternoon of December 20, 1989—
"Never mind that I only did a page plus—I started."

At the plaque ceremony, the Biographer asked his colleagues why *Clarel*—the two-volume epic poem Melville composed at this address—was not included on the plaque.

"Because we couldn't include *everything*," answered the secretary-treasurer of the society—
"For the general public, we thought that *Billy Budd* would be his most familiar work."

The outgoing president noted that *Billy Budd* was not published during Melville's lifetime, and the incoming president added that it was not published until 1924.

Someone with a question about Melville's work as a customs inspector was referred to the Melvillean known among his colleagues as "the Custom House expert."

Initially Melville walked from Twenty-Sixth Street to his post on the Hudson River, the expert explained, but when his post was moved uptown to the East River, he probably took the elevated train—
"It's strange to think of this man, who once sailed in square-rigged ships, riding the El."

Melville worked nineteen years at his low-level position, refusing bribes, surviving political purges, and never receiving a raise—
"It's mind-boggling," said the Custom House expert, "Melville wearing a uniform that was just like a city policeman's."

Biographers have little to say about the thousands of hours he spent inspecting ships for contraband, collecting fees and mail, and filing written reports.

"It was not savory work," one writes.

Melville's career as a customs inspector was longer than his prose career, longer than his friendship with Hawthorne, longer than his residence at Arrowhead, longer than his son Malcolm's life.

Shortly after Melville's retirement in 1885, at age sixty-six, his second son, Stanwix, died after years of drifting, disappointment, and malady.

(Stannie, they called him.)

According to his death certificate, Stanwix died "in the 35th year of his age," which perhaps explains why two recent Melville biographers erroneously state that he died at thirty-five.

One writes that he died in Sacramento, which appears to be wrong. One writes that he died alone in a hotel room, which also appears to be wrong.

(And what of my own errors of transmission, of transcription? And what difference could they make?)

No matter the particulars of Stanwix's death—it appears that he died in a San Francisco hospital at age thirty-four—his life did not meet its expectancy, and it did not work.

His long list of Grand Ideas included sheep farming and dentistry— "Fate is against me in most of my undertakings," he once wrote.

Lizzie was devastated by the news of her son's death— "She is in great trouble," reported Melville's sister Helen, "and seems unable to find solace for her grief."

"The sorrows that lie round our paths as we grow older!"

For his part, Melville is said to have been stoic about Stanwix's death, though numerous scholars have suggested that *Billy Budd*, his late return to prose, was a reckoning with the deaths of his sons.

In the final five years of his life, he painstakingly developed the brief prose headnote to his poem "Billy in the Darbies" into a 351-page manuscript, unfinished at his death.

"[A] last will and testament," Elizabeth Hardwick calls *Billy Budd*, in which the eponymous young sailor forgives the captain who condemns him to death.

Another biographer calls it a "personal confession and catharsis," an "'inside narrative' of Malcolm's death, and perhaps an acknowledgment that he had driven away Stanwix, too."

According to a third biographer, Melville kept revising and expanding *Billy Budd* "as if he could not bear to let it go."

This morning I see that late last night my husband sent me a link to the Sopranos arguing at the dinner table about whether or not *Billy Budd* is "a gay book," and a link to Morrissey singing "Billy Budd" (with Spanish subtitles) in the Hammerstein Ballroom, and a link to a scene of William Shatner playing Billy Budd in a live performance on the CBC in 1955.

My husband is on his second day of quarantine in our partially finished basement—
"Regrettably a member of our team who you interacted with on Monday, February 22nd has tested positive for COVID-19."

Dad's not going to die, I keep telling our younger daughter.

He's not going to *die*, her older sister says, unconsolingly.

I'm not going to die, he told her last night on family Zoom.

When the girls wandered off he asked to see my breasts in case he died.

I also screen-shared with him the digitized manuscript of *Billy Budd* available through Harvard's Houghton Library.

Page after foxed page.

Pages x-ed out with crayons, pages with scraps affixed, pages with six different page numbers, pages in two colors of ink with penciled corrections, pages cut in pieces.

Herman Melville used crayons? my husband said.

He asked me for a bowl of cereal and the dog.

Don't die, please, I called down the stairs.

After Melville died, Lizzie attempted to collate and annotate the chaotic manuscript, which only made matters more confusing for early editors of *Billy Budd*, who mistook her handwriting for Melville's.

She stored the manuscript in a tin bread box where it remained for twenty-eight years—"a literary near-death experience"—until Melville's granddaughter shared it with Raymond Weaver, Melville's first biographer.

Remarkably I can find no image of this bread box, which I've seen described as "japanned."

One reviewer on Tripadvisor mentions that it was "great to see" the bread box in the Herman Melville Memorial Room at the Berkshire Athenaeum, but doesn't describe it.

Billy Budd emerged from this bread box in 1924, in an edition transcribed and edited by Raymond Weaver.

Although Weaver regarded the novel as "not distinguished," other readers hailed it as a major work—
In *Aspects of the Novel* (1927), E. M. Forster wrote that Melville in *Billy Budd* "reaches straight back into the universal, to a blackness and sadness so transcending our own that they are undistinguishable from glory."

Albert Camus called it a "flawless story" and Thomas Mann called it "the most beautiful story in the world."

As it happens, the editions of *Billy Budd* that Forster, Camus, and Mann celebrated would have been riddled with significant errors of transcription and editing—
It was not until 1962 that a standard and reliable edition of *Billy Budd* appeared.

Legendary Melvillean Harrison Hayford and a colleague had spent ten years studying the bread-box manuscript to understand Melville's intentions and to correct the errors of previous editions.

Hayford used a process called "genetic editing," which aims to create a "healthy" text by rooting out "cancerous" elements that have been transmitted from edition to edition, like bad genes.

An unhealthy text can infect scholarship—

In a chapter of his foundational book *American Renaissance*, F. O. Matthiessen made much of Melville's phrase *soiled fish of the sea.*

"Hardly anyone but Melville," Matthiessen wrote, "could have created the shudder that results" from this unexpected description—It "could only have sprung from an imagination that had apprehended the terrors of the deep."

But what Melville wrote in *White-Jacket* was not "soiled fish of the sea" but *coiled fish of the sea.*

Eight years later a graduate student at Ohio State published a brief note in a major academic journal, gently correcting "soiled" to "coiled" and calling Matthiessen a "victim of a rather unlucky error" made by "some unknown typesetter."

In a 2011 lecture archived on YouTube, a UVA English professor notes that the confusion between the two words "is funny, but it's also very sad"—
"Not primarily because of this—but with this as a contributing factor—within the year of this error being pointed out, Professor Matthiessen committed suicide."

Matthiessen, at age forty-eight, jumped from the twelfth floor of a Boston hotel on April Fool's Day 1950.

In 1950, Melville scholarship was, according to Harrison Hayford, "an absurd situation"—
"For all this close reading, all this study, nobody had ever thought to see if the texts themselves were reliable."

To produce a "healthy" edition of a Melville text, Hayford and his colleagues had to compare each page of each existing edition, working backward to find malignant typographical variants.

Tell me about the Hinman Collator, said my husband, healthy but bored on his fourth day of basement quarantine.

It was invented by Charlton Hinman, I told him, speaking quietly into the phone so I did not wake our daughter in the next room.

Hinman, I said, was a literary scholar and former Navy code breaker who wanted to find a more efficient way to cross-reference pages from printings of Shakespeare's First Folio.

His wife said he was a tinkerer—he once made croquet mallets on his wood lathe.

The old way of comparing texts, I told my husband because I knew he would like it, was called the "Wimbledon method."

Hinman's prototype, I told him because I knew he would like it, was built out of two projectors, pieces of an apple crate, some cardboard, and parts of an Erector Set that he swiped from a friend's son.

In its final form the Hinman Collator was six feet tall and more than four hundred pounds—
Hinman said it was kind of awesome but also kind of ludicrous.

Having found an image on the internet, my husband said it made him believe we could beat the Russians to the moon.

He asked me how it works and I said lights and mirrors.

I told him that the Royal Canadian Mounted Police borrowed a Hinman from the University of New Brunswick to investigate forgeries.

And that after a potentially catastrophic hyphen error, a pharmaceutical company bought one to help proofread prescription labels.

I told him that the CIA arranged for a clandestine cash purchase of a Hinman on a remote loading dock.

And that several years later the agency inquired about the purchase of another one—apparently the CIA had stored the machine in a location so secret that even the CIA did not know where it was.

I told my husband that there's a scholar who has tracked down forty-one of the fifty-seven or fifty-eight or fifty-nine Hinman Collators that he estimates were produced.

He suspects that the lost collators are gone for good, I said, but doesn't rule out the possibility that another may be found.

That's a big thing to lose, my husband said.

What's the biggest thing you've ever lost? he asked me.

From bed I regarded, as I often do, the sliver of night where the curtains meet.

Or rather, don't, quite.

I meant the biggest object, he said, the biggest object you've ever lost.

Probably my bike, I said.

He said that was stolen, not lost.

I said maybe my ski jacket.

My husband told me about the time he left his car in neutral outside of a convenience store and when he came out it had rolled to the other side of the parking lot and he couldn't find it and then our daughter came in and asked if I was talking to Dad.

I handed her the phone and she began to pace the room in the manner of her father, speaking furtively in the manner of her father, as if to prevent eavesdropping.

Eventually it became clear that they were discussing Taylor Swift's album *evermore.*

This morning I see that in 1961 Ohio State purchased the twelfth Hinman Collator for work on scholarly editions of Hawthorne.

And that in 1965 Northwestern purchased the eighteenth Hinman Collator for Harrison Hayford's work as general editor of *The Writings of Herman Melville*—
Hayford estimated that it would take his team four years to complete definitive, healthy versions of all of Melville's work.

Seventeen years later, after extensive editorial and financial challenges, just six of the anticipated fifteen volumes had been published, though Hayford was hopeful that the project would be complete in three more years, at the time of his retirement.

The final book of the series was published in 2017, fifty-two years after the project began and fifteen years after Hayford's death.

God keep me from ever completing anything.

Harrison Hayford carrying with him a photocopy of Melville's hand-writing; Harrison Hayford writing in the margins of library books with his characteristic brown pencil; Harrison Hayford picking up pennies on the street, his eyes, he said, sharpened by his work as a textual editor; Harrison Hayford advising students to "have something in every single sentence for the reader"; Harrison Hayford advising a student to study Melville, not Henry James; Harrison Hayford advising a student to study Melville, not Shakespeare; Harrison Hayford asking students who had earned their Ph.D.s to call him "Harry"; Harrison Hayford collaborating with graduate students but refusing to include his name; Harrison Hayford needing a ride to the bookstore because he didn't have a driver's license; Harrison Hayford "bookstoring" in Chicago on Sunday nights; Harrison Hayford and his thousands and thousands of books, his bags of books, his shelves of books, his basement of books, his book-buying and book-lending and book-giving; Harrison Hayford selling fifty thousand books to a Japanese university; Harrison Hayford buying a three-dollar used book when he couldn't find anything good so the bookseller would continue to look after him; Harrison Hayford loading up his arms with books on sexuality, determined to figure out for himself whether Melville was homosexual; Harrison Hayford looking through the Hinman Collator for the first time, seeing a *y* wagging its tail . . .

No one, said one scholar, did more "basic work" on Melville than Hayford—
"If there is an afterlife, I'd like to think Melville would be waiting there to shake his hand and thank him," the director of Northwestern University Press said upon his death.

("The family has asked that any contributions in Hayford's memory be made to the newly established Melville Archive and Cultural Center.")

The Melville Log, the Melville Revival, the Melville Industry, the Melville Society, the Melville Vortex, the Melville Room, the Melville Effect . . .

"There is no closure," said one of Hayford's most prominent former students.

"There is no end in sight," said that prominent former student's prominent former student.

Just five more days, my husband said last night.

This morning I'm unable to access HawMel-db, a searchable database created by a college student at Bard–Simon's Rock in 1999.

She created this database after extensive research into the relationship between Hawthorne and Melville, her chosen topic for a class assignment.

The student's "Hawthorne and Melville Inquiry Log," however, is available online and provides the outcomes of some of her database searches:

Was Melville's love for Hawthorne unrequited?

YES: 3 sources

NO: 6 sources

Was the relationship between Hawthorne and Melville non-Platonic?

YES: 7

NO: 5

Was Melville part of the reason Hawthorne moved from the Berkshires?

YES: 6

NO: 3

Was there an estrangement between Hawthorne and Melville at the end of their relationship?

YES: 2

NO: 5

One of the sources the student found most useful was her ILL copy of Harrison Hayford's 1945 dissertation "Melville and Hawthorne: A Biographical and Critical Study"—

She was so engrossed by Hayford's study that she read it in a day, finishing it in her car outside of Price Chopper.

The dissertation was particularly helpful because it listed all known meetings between Hawthorne and Melville from 1850 to 1851—

Eight or nine, depending on how one delineates a meeting.

If you spend the night at someone's house and the next day that person comes back with you to your house to spend the night, is that one meeting or two?

(That's one, my husband said.)

Although he couldn't prove it, Hayford speculated that Melville and Hawthorne met an additional time, in November 1851, when Melville would have presented Hawthorne with a copy of *Moby-Dick*, dedicated to him "in admiration of his genius."

"This episode," Hayford added in a footnote, "is purely conjectural."

This meeting remained conjectural, though plausible, for forty-seven years until the summer of 1992 when it was confirmed, in a triumphant feat of archival research, by Hayford's former student Hershel Parker.

The Biographer.

Putting out his hand.

This morning I see that in the summer of 1987 he was in the Boston Public Library, searching microfilm of Massachusetts newspapers for reviews of *Moby-Dick*, when he came across an article in the *Lowell Weekly Journal and Courier*, published December 19, 1851, and reprinted from a longer version in the *Windsor Journal*.

The article, a dispatch written by an anonymous special correspondent from the Vermont newspaper, describes the Lenox cottage of the famous literary recluse Nathaniel Hawthorne.

Determined to see the original version, as well as any other dispatches from this special correspondent, the Biographer typed a note into his large computer file on the year 1851: "MUST FIND WINDSOR VT. JOURNAL."

At the Library of Congress he was informed that the *Journal* "was not extant anywhere," so he enlisted a student in New England to search Vermont libraries, and asked a Portsmouth historian to put the newspaper "on his hunting list."

Eventually the historian tracked down the *Windsor Journal* and in August 1992 he sent the Biographer a packet containing photocopies of articles written by the special correspondent—
"At 2 pm mail & all hell broke loose," the Biographer noted in his diary.

Contained in the packet was a second dispatch from the correspondent, documenting a meeting between Melville and Hawthorne at a Lenox hotel—
"Not very long ago, the author of the 'Scarlet Letter' and the author of 'Typee,' having, in some unaccountable way, gotten a mutual desire to see one another, as if neither had a home to which he could invite the other, made arrangements in a very formal manner to dine together at a hotel in this village."

"What a solemn time they must have had," the correspondent wrote, "those mighty conjurers in the domain of the imagination, all alone in the dining room of a hotel!"

The Biographer read the photocopied article with shaking hands—Here was the meeting that Hayford had imagined almost fifty years ago.

"Jesus," he wrote in his diary, "*my mind is wild.*"

He sat at his computer and deleted his old note to himself: "MUST FIND WINDSOR VT. *JOURNAL.*"

Next, he shared the news with Jay Leyda, whose *The Melville Log* he had for years been updating and augmenting with the expectation of publishing a multivolume third edition called *The New Melville Log.*

Leyda, who had been dead four and a half years, was, according to the Biographer, "the only dead scholar I talked to."

"Wanted a drink," he wrote in his diary, although he had forsworn alcohol six years earlier so that he could remain optimally alert as he attempted to finish both *The New Melville Log* and his biography.

(The *Log* remains unpublished—as of 2018, the Biographer's Melville file, his "archive of archives," was nine thousand pages.)

In lieu of a celebratory drink he called Hayford, then Maurice Sendak, and then "went back to work."

Eventually the Biographer realized that his biography would have to be divided into two volumes, each one longer than the proposed whole, and he faced the question of where to split the life.

"You don't have any choice," a fellow Melvillean told him—
"You have to end it in the hotel."

The final chapter of the first volume, "Melville in Triumph," indeed concludes with Melville's meeting with Hawthorne at the Lenox hotel, on perhaps November 14, a Friday, the official publication date of *Moby-Dick*.

It was, according to the Biographer, "a sacred occasion in American literary life."

"At some well-chosen moment," he wrote, "Melville took out the book whose publication they had both been awaiting and handed his friend an inscribed copy."

The Biographer's rendering of this occasion "breaks into SONG," Harrison Hayford wrote in the margin of a draft.

(Some readers, however, have described it as "largely imagined," "charming and fabricated," a "fantasy.")

In the Biographer's account, Hawthorne was "profoundly moved" by Melville's gift.

Enveloped in tobacco smoke, the two men, the Biographer wrote, "lingered long after the dining room had emptied, each reverential toward the other's genius, each aware that when they met again, in West Newton, in Boston, or wherever their Fates might bring them together, they would not fall at once into these present terms of intimacy."

"Take it all in all," Volume 1 concludes, "this was the happiest day of Melville's life."

The claim seems dubious, but last night I couldn't figure out if the problem lies in the selection of this particular day out of all of Melville's many days, or if it lies in the presumption to assess the happiest day in the life of someone else, particularly someone so mysterious and dead, or if it lies in the potential confusion of happiest with other superlatives such as most content or most consequential or most memorable, or if it lies in the belief in the very concept of a happiest day of a life.

I lay awake, thinking of some of the happy days of my life, but the thought that any one of them might be the happiest day of my life I found unhappy.

Of course I didn't like the idea that on the happiest day of Melville's life, his wife was at home nursing their newborn son despite suffering from a breast infection so painful the walls in her room had been draped with sheets because the pattern of the wallpaper made her dizzy.

Some of my happy days were nights—
in our nursery, reading *Howards End*.

(You don't have any choice, you have to end it in the nursery.)

That small room had a Dutch door, I remember.

From its window I could see, when the leaves were down, the northeast corner of the hayfield, its birds dropping and lifting like thoughts.

If my husband had been with me last night I might have woken him up with a hand on his back and told him that awful story about Lizzie and the wallpaper or, because I knew he would like it, a scholar's sweet memory of Harrison Hayford calling the Chicago White Sox the Great White Sox or the Biographer's extraordinary claim about Melville's happiest day or John Updike's allegation somewhere that Hawthorne was at his happiest in the Berkshires though he didn't know it or my suspicion that I must not understand anything at all about happiness or my eager anticipation of the forthcoming first biography of Elizabeth Hardwick or Maurice Sendak's refusal to find out the age of his German shepherd, Herman, because he didn't want to know and in fact wished he didn't know his own age or my heretical paraphrase of Mary Ruefle's poem "My Happiness," in which the speaker's happiness follows a porcupine into a culvert.

If my husband had been there I might not have lain in the dark attempting to calculate the number of days Herman Melville lived, but then again I might have.

The number I derived—inaccurate, but not wildly, it turns out—meant nothing, then anything, then one thing.

[*sic vita est*]

I once, like other spoonies, cherished a loose sort of notion that I did not care to live very long, wrote Herman Melville at age forty-three— It's easy to find this passage in *The Letters of Herman Melville* because Melville drew a skull and crossbones.

By the way, Death, in my skull, seems to tip a knowing sort of wink out of his left eye, he wrote parenthetically.

What does that mean, I wonder?

A spoony, I see, is archaic British slang, meaning a fool or simpleton— derived perhaps from the shallowness of a spoon.

And I see it was not Updike but Paul Auster who wrote that the summer before Hawthorne moved away from the Berkshires was "the best moment of his life, whether he knew it or not."

"Looking back on Hawthorne's career now, and knowing that he would be dead just thirteen years later (a few weeks short of his sixtieth birthday), that season in Lenox stands out as one of the happiest periods of his life, a moment of sublime equipoise and fulfillment."

The Hawthornes left Lenox in a snowstorm on November 21, one week after Melville and Hawthorne dined in the hotel—Melville's "publication party," the Biographer calls it, "to which he invited a solitary guest."

Hawthorne appears to have read *Moby-Dick* in two days, sitting in his study while his wife packed the house and took care of their three young children, nursing the infant, Rose.

"What a book Melville has written!" he wrote to a mutual friend weeks later.

The letter he wrote to Melville about the book—likely destroyed by Melville—is the unlocated item most desired by Melvilleans.

"Imagine the auction value," the Biographer wrote, "especially if Melville made on it any notes for his reply!"

Melville's reply the next day was, according to a Hawthorne biographer, "one of the most extraordinarily intimate letters one author ever sent another."

Why don't you read it to me, my husband said last night on the phone.

I don't know, I said.

It's kind of intense, I said.

I told him it was easy to find online.

Just read it to me, he said.

It was late—
It felt too late for Melville's precipice, but my husband doesn't ask for much.

He requires a lot, but he doesn't ask for much.

M y dear Hawthorne, I said to my husband.

People think that if a man has undergone any hardship, he should have a reward; but for my part, if I have done the hardest possible day's work, and then come to sit down in a corner and eat my supper comfortably—why, then I don't think I deserve any reward for my hard day's work—for am I not now at peace? Is not my supper good? My peace and my supper are my reward, my dear Hawthorne.

Hold on, my husband said, let me turn off the dryer.

So, I said, your joy-giving and exultation-breeding letter is not my reward for my ditcher's work with that book, but is the good goddess's bonus over and above what was stipulated for—for not one man in five cycles, who is wise, will expect appreciative recognition from his fellows, or any one of them. Appreciation! Recognition! Is Jove appreciated? Why, ever since Adam, who has got to the meaning of his great allegory—the world? Then we pigmies must be content to have our paper allegories but ill comprehended. I say your appreciation is my glorious gratuity. In my proud, humble way,—a shepherd-king,—I was lord of a little vale in the solitary Crimea; but you have now given me the crown of India. But on trying it on my head, I found it fell down on my ears, notwithstanding their asinine length—for it's only such ears that sustain such crowns. Your letter was handed me last night on the road going to Mr. Morewood's, and I read it there. Had I been at home, I would have sat down at once and answered it.

Melville was on his way to a party that night, I explained, and so he probably had Hawthorne's letter in his pocket all evening, as he spoke irreverently about religion to one of the guests and as his lot was drawn in the contest to name three of his neighbor's cows.

My husband wanted to know what he named them, and I said Molly, Polly, and Dolly.

Keep going, my husband said.

In me divine magnanimities are spontaneous and instantaneous—catch them while you can. The world goes round, and the other side comes up. So now I can't write what I felt. But I felt pantheistic then—your heart beat in my ribs and mine in yours, and both in God's. A sense of unspeakable security is in me this moment, on account of your having understood the book. I have written a wicked book, and feel spotless as the lamb. Ineffable socialities are in me. I would sit down and dine with you and all the gods in old Rome's Pantheon. It is a strange feeling—no hopefulness is in it, no despair. Content—that is it; and irresponsibility; but without licentious inclination. I speak now of my profoundest sense of being, not of an incidental feeling. Whence come you, Hawthorne? By what right do you drink from my flagon of life? And when I put it to my lips—lo, they are yours and not mine.

My husband's low whistle during this passage was not lewd but amazed.

I feel that the Godhead is broken up like the bread at the Supper, I said, and that we are the pieces. Hence this infinite fraternity of feeling. Now, sympathizing with the paper, my angel turns over another page. You did not care a penny for the book. But, now and then as you read, you understood the pervading thought that impelled the book—and that you praised. Was it not so? You were archangel enough to despise the imperfect body, and embrace the soul. Once you hugged the ugly Socrates because you saw the flame in the mouth, and heard the rushing of the demon,—the familiar,—and recognized the sound; for you have heard it in your own solitudes.

Solitudes, my husband said.

Hawthorne would have been fine with quarantine, I told him.

He probably would have liked it, I said.

Haven't you, I said, liked it, a little bit, being down there?

Only a little, he said.

He said he wouldn't have liked it if he were alone.

My dear Hawthorne, the atmospheric skepticisms steal into me now, and make me doubtful of my sanity in writing you thus. But, believe me, I am not mad, most noble Festus! But truth is ever incoherent, and when the big hearts strike together, the concussion is a little stunning. Farewell. Don't write a word about the book. That would be robbing me of my miserly delight. I am heartily sorry I ever wrote anything about you—it was paltry.

It wasn't paltry, I said to my husband, it was twenty-six handwritten pages.

And he really shouldn't have told Hawthorne not to write about
Moby-Dick—
He was in serious debt when he wrote the letter, and any word from Hawthorne would have helped the book.

I said that the Biographer, who claims he's been talking out loud to Melville for over fifty years, often asks him with anguish, "Ah, why did you do that?"

Lord, I said, when shall we be done growing? As long as we have anything more to do, we have done nothing. So, now, let us add Moby Dick to our blessing, and step from that. Leviathan is not the biggest fish;—I have heard of Krakens.

Oh god, my husband said, *Pierre*.

This is a long letter, I said.

Are you saying that or is Melville? my husband asked.

Melville, I said. This is a long letter, but you are not at all bound to answer it. Possibly, if you do answer it, and direct it to Herman Melville, you will missend it—for the very fingers that now guide this pen are not precisely the same that just took it up and put it on this paper. Lord, when shall we be done changing? Ah! it's a long stage, and no inn in sight, and night coming, and the body cold. But with you for a passenger, I am content and can be happy. I shall leave the world, I feel, with more satisfaction for having come to know you. Knowing you persuades me more than the Bible of our immortality.

C x 1, a little.

Is this your favorite Melville? my husband asked me.

I said I also liked Melville pointing with his cane to an engraved seascape and telling his granddaughter, "See the little boats sailing hither and thither."

Probably my favorite Melville, I said, is Melville in the barn, feeding his cow.

He said that was a good Melville.

I said, What a pity, that, for your plain, bluff letter, you should get such gibberish! Mention me to Mrs. Hawthorne and to the children, and so, good-by to you, with my blessing. Herman.

It's the only time he signed a letter "Herman" to someone who wasn't a member of his family—
That we know of, I said.

I think it was then, before the postcripts, that my husband said he missed us, that he had liked listening to our voices at dinner.

Our muffled voices—often he couldn't even hear what we were saying, he said.

He said the sound of our voices made him happy.

He thanked me for reading the letter and said he'd see us soon.

P.S., I said, I can't stop yet.

(My husband's laughter.)

If the world was entirely made up of Magians, I'll tell you what I should do. I should have a paper-mill established at one end of the house, and so have an endless riband of foolscap rolling in upon my desk; and upon that endless riband I should write a thousand—a million—billion thoughts, all under the form of a letter to you. The divine magnet is in you, and my magnet responds. Which is the biggest? A foolish question—they are *One*.

(My husband's silence.)

Signed H, I said.

There's another postscript, I said.

(My husband's profanity.)

Don't think that by writing me a letter, you shall always be bored with an immediate reply to it—and so keep both of us delving over a writing-desk eternally. No such thing! I sha'n't always answer your letters, and you may do just as you please.

(My husband's bon voyage.)

P.S. I couldn't *sleep*.

It occurred to me that I had never shown my husband the moss that Melville pasted into his copy of Hawthorne's *Mosses from an Old Manse*, so I texted him a screenshot.

I thought he'd see it in the morning but he was still awake—
Is that seaweed? he texted.

I texted, Its [sic] moss—
at 1:34 a.m., I see.

I saw his typing bubbles, so I transcribed the inscription Melville wrote beneath the moss.

And then transcribed Melville's postscript to his inscription.

My husband's typing bubbles disappeared, then reappeared.

There's a lot I could have typed.

That Melville reread *Mosses from an Old Manse* a year after Hawthorne's death.

That next to one passage he wrote, "Nothing can be finer than this."

That Melville had a habit of writing in books as he read them.

That Susan Howe called his annotations conversations with the dead.

That one scholar is trying to edit and display all of Melville's annotations, even the ones that were mysteriously erased.

That that scholar meant to study Byron and Shelley but fell into what he calls the Melville Vortex.

That he's also trying to recover Melville's large personal library, an estimated one thousand volumes.

That Melville bought books when he was broke and when he was dying, that he bought books as gifts for family members that he wanted for himself.

That Lizzie probably didn't want *Walks About the City and Environs of Jerusalem* for Christmas 1870.

My mom would have liked that moss, my husband texted.

> Yes, thought of her too.
> Those plastic bins of bark and seed pods

Feathers.

> Chestnuts

Fucking rocks.

> Remember her on the ladder looking at that cocoon

That ladder is terrible.

I think she had her ipad?

She did.
She was up there for like an hour.

Her tremor was already bad.

How old was Hawthorne?
When he died.

59 only

When did Melville last see him?
Not sure.
I'll find out
Tomorrow I mean
I mean today

My husband signed off with a string of emojis intended, I think, to depict the relationship between Melville and Hawthorne.

Then a yawning face, a spouting whale, and a heart.

I stand for the heart, Melville once wrote to Hawthorne—
To the dogs with the head!

I wanted to find out the last time the two men saw each other but instead I tried Patti Smith's cure for insomnia.

I lay on the cold bathroom floor and imagined I was a sailor on a whaling ship during a raging storm.

When the captain's son caught his foot in some rope and was pulled overboard, I dove into the violent sea to save him.

With one hand I clasped the boy and with the other a life rope, and we were pulled by the other men back to the ship's deck.

The captain invited me to his cabin, where he embraced me and asked how he could repay me.

I asked for a full serving of rum for each of the sailors.

The captain complied but asked again what he could do for me.

I told him it had been a long time since I had slept in a bed, and he offered me his.

I stared at the captain's bed, its down pillows, its soft blanket.

(Here I got off the bathroom floor and walked back to my own bed.)

I imagined saying a prayer, blowing out candles, and falling into grateful sleep.

Eventually morning arrived, or I arrived at morning, and I learned that the last time Melville saw Hawthorne was in 1857, seven years before Hawthorne's death.

The two men met just three times after their dinner in the Lenox hotel when Melville presented Hawthorne with a dedication copy of *Moby-Dick*—
the most extended of which took place five years later in Liverpool, where Hawthorne was serving as American consul.

Melville, age thirty-seven, had recently completed *The Confidence-Man*, his final work of prose appearing in his lifetime.

Funded by an advance on Lizzie's inheritance, he had embarked on a six-month tour of Europe and the Holy Land designed to restore his health (and to provide his family a respite from his moods and habits).

"I suppose you have been informed by some of the family, how very ill, Herman has been," Judge Shaw wrote to his son—
He "overworks himself & brings on severe nervous affections."

When Melville showed up unannounced at the consulate in Liverpool, he looked, according to Hawthorne, "much as he used to do (a little paler, and perhaps a little sadder)."

In his journal Hawthorne reported that Melville had told him that "he did not anticipate much pleasure in his rambles, for that the spirit of adventure is gone out of him."

During Melville's stay with the Hawthornes, the two men took a long walk by the Irish Sea.

Hawthorne recorded that they "sat down in a hollow among the sand hills (sheltering ourselves from the high, cool wind) and smoked a cigar."

"Melville, as he always does, began to reason of Providence and futurity, and of everything that lies beyond human ken, and informed me that he had 'pretty much made up his mind to be annihilated'; but still he does not seem to rest in that anticipation; and, I think, will never rest until he gets hold of a definite belief."

"It is strange how he persists—and has persisted ever since I knew him, and probably long before—in wandering to-and-fro over these deserts, as dismal and monotonous as the sand hills amid which we were sitting."

"If he were a religious man, he would be one of the most truly religious and reverential; he has a very high and noble nature, and better worth immortality than most of us."

Sands & grass, Melville recorded in his journal. *Wild & desolate. A strong wind. Good talk.*

This outing might be considered an earthly version of the Heaven that Melville described to Hawthorne in a letter five years earlier— *If ever, my dear Hawthorne, in the eternal times that are to come, you and I shall sit down in Paradise, in some little shady corner by ourselves; and if we shall by any means be able to smuggle a basket of champagne there (I won't believe in a Temperance Heaven), and if we shall then cross our celestial legs in the celestial grass that is forever tropical, and strike our glasses and our heads together, till both musically ring in concert,—then, O my dear fellow-mortal, how shall we pleasantly discourse of all the things manifold which now so distress us,—when all the earth shall be but a reminiscence, yea, its final dissolution an antiquity.*

In his next sentence Melville imagined the *comic songs* composed in Paradise:
> *Oh, when I lived in that queer little hole called the world*
> *Oh, when I toiled and sweated below*
> *Oh, when I knocked and was knocked in the fight*

This morning I had two voice memos from my husband.

The second one instructed me to delete the first, a two-minute folk song about "that queer little hole called the world."

He'd composed it on our daughter's forsaken guitar.

In one column: the things I want from my husband.
In another: the things I get.

> Here the cigars are celestial
> and our words unfurl
> Above the queer little hole called the world

During the Bad Time my husband and I disagreed about moving to another state, to this one.

I lost.
It's an art, according to Elizabeth Bishop.

("Then practice losing farther, losing faster")

On our first wedding anniversary in our new home, my husband gave me three plants: Solomon's seal, bloodroot, and primrose.

In his card—which why can't I find this card?—he explained that these plants were cuttings from cuttings from plants in the Dickinson Homestead gardens—
He'd acquired them from a local gardener who had surreptitiously taken cuttings from Emily's gardens years earlier.

Our dog dug out the primrose several years ago, but the Solomon's seal and bloodroot have done well.

Any day now we should see the first buds.

When I came downstairs my husband was standing at the peninsula, consuming *a certain amount of oxygen*, as Melville put it in his skull &

crossbones letter, *which unconsumed might create some subtle disturbance in Nature.*

He had a beard, a travel mug, and a duffel bag.

He had a creased photo of our children feeding bison.

I told him my library books are due, and can't be renewed.

Hello, my life, he said—
It's something he says to me.
It's from a Grace Paley story.

Searching for that story, called "Wants," I found this evening my husband's paperback copy of Paley's collected stories.

It so happens that his copy is inscribed:

FOR CHRIS

GRACE PALEY

THANKS FOR OUR

TALKING.

SEE YOU?

I had forgotten that my husband interviewed Grace Paley at a literary festival in Western Massachusetts.

And forgotten that I didn't attend because I had a one-year-old and was seven months pregnant.

And forgotten that Grace Paley died of cancer less than two months after my husband met her.

After she wrote, "See you?"

One hour of my life was spent in her life, said my husband, whom I found back in the basement, wearing safety goggles.

He said lucky him.

Grace Paley died in 2007 at age eighty-four.

Her *New York Times* obituary, I see this morning, contains a lengthy passage from "Wants."

"Hello, my life," the narrator says to her ex-husband, to whom she was married for twenty-seven years.

She's sitting on the steps of the library—
Her Edith Wharton novels are eighteen years overdue even though she lives two blocks away.

"Because I don't understand how time passes," she explains.

"Time's quaint stream," writes Dickinson.
"Time's wily Chargers," writes Dickinson.

Life is a long Dardenelles, writes Melville.
Life is so short, and so ridiculous and irrational, writes Melville.

"Look at Melville's eighty long years of writhing," wrote D. H. Lawrence, though Melville did not writhe for eighty years.

He died in 1891 at the age of seventy-two.

In the first hour of September 28, a Monday.

"The poor man is out of his suffering," his niece wrote, "and we can not but rejoice for him."

(The cause of death, Lizzie later recorded in her 1866 pocket diary, was "enlargement of the heart.")

Melville in his late years seems to have found relief from the writhing—
"He grew calmer and quieter," according to a granddaughter, "grew mellower," according to a biographer.

He grew roses—
sent dried petals in letters.

I shall always try and have a rose-leaf reserved for you, be the season what it may, he wrote to Lizzie's cousin in 1885.

At the end of that year he retired from the custom house after nineteen years of service.

Melville's primary occupations in retirement were reading, writing, walking the city, and browsing bookstores with his $25 monthly book allowance from Lizzie.

A bookstore employee remembered that he "walked with a rapid stride and almost a sprightly gait."

He wore a black felt hat and "almost invariably" a blue suit.

He was "preceded by a beard that was impressive even for those hirsute days."

He was considered a misanthrope by many—"damn fools" was his frequent epithet—though some characterized him as shy, elusive, and self-effacing.

To Julian Hawthorne, Melville would not speak of the "red-cottage days."

To friends and acquaintances, he would not speak of his novels— "I have forgotten them," he told one friend.

When another asked to borrow them, Melville claimed he did not own a single copy.

"My books will speak for themselves," he once said.

His late years were, according to John Updike, "public silence and private poetry."

In retirement he paid to publish two volumes of poetry in editions of twenty-five copies each.

One of which did not include his name on the title page.

His study, like the one at Arrowhead, faced north— "bleakly north," his granddaughter Eleanor wrote.

To her it was "a place of mystery and awe" that she never entered unless invited.

A dark room, a room "to be fled"— dark bed, dark desk, "high dim book-case, topped by strange plaster heads."

On the table covered with papers she knew not to touch there was a bag of figs, "and one of the pieces of sweet stickiness was for me."

Grandpa, his granddaughters called him.

"I often wondered what grandpa could be doing for hours on end in his study," Frances wrote.

On the rare instances she was invited in, she was permitted to play with the interesting items on his desk—candlestick, pincushion, rolling ruler.

"There was no wall space at all," she recalled, "just books, books, books."

She used them to build houses on the floor—"A set of Schopenhauer pleased me most—they were not too heavy to handle and of a nice palish blue color."

More often they met their grandfather in Lizzie's room—"a very different place—sunny, comfortable and familiar, with a sewing machine and a *white* bed like other people's."

There they sat on their grandfather's lap, patted and squeezed his beard, which Eleanor remembered as "tight curled like the horse hair breaking out of old upholstered chairs, firm and wiry to the grasp, and squarely chopped."

They listened to his outlandish tales of islands and cannibals, unaware that they were true, or mostly true.

Melville thought his granddaughters would eventually "turn against him," as their mother had, but they never did, and neither did his wife.

When, after Melville's death, a family member suggested to Elizabeth Melville that her life might be easier and happier, "an almost fierce pride that she had been Herman's wife silenced the imprudent tongue."

(A hidden panel of her desk, a carved message: "To know all is to forgive all.")

She used black-bordered mourning stationery for more than two years after he died.

She saved a packet of his love letters until her death, at which point it was destroyed—
(Imagine the auction value, wrote no one at all.)

The library of her new apartment was filled with her husband's furniture, books, papers, and art.

His portrait hung above the mantel.

The bread box containing *Billy Budd* sat on his writing table.

(Affixed to the underside of that table, according to Eleanor, was a piece of paper on which Melville, quoting Schiller, had written, *Keep true to the dreams of thy youth*.)

A decade after her husband's death, Lizzie was still inviting guests to her library in order to generate interest in his books and papers.

Throughout the fifteen years that she outlived Melville, she worked to rehabilitate his literary reputation—
"For the desire of my heart has been to see my husband's books resurrected, as it were, to call forth as they have begun to do, the recognition which their birthright might reasonably claim," she wrote to Arthur Stedman, Melville's literary executor.

She and Stedman successfully advocated for the reissue of *Typee*, *Omoo*, *White-Jacket*, and *Moby-Dick*.

Additionally, Lizzie collected reviews, managed copyrights, edited manuscripts, wrote and corrected biographical material, and corresponded with publishers and literary figures.

"Lizzie as 'first Melvillean,'" this sticky note says.

The so-called Melville Revival of the 1920s was based substantially upon Elizabeth Melville's work, though scholars have been slow to give her credit—
"Melville studies," one recent article asserts, "is built on a history of women's labor that has largely been erased and, when recognized, discounted."

"Unacknowledged precursor," says this sticky note.

"Elizabeth's LEGWORK," this one says.

This one says, "Melville's scrivener."

And this one, "under under unfavorable circumstances."

Elizabeth Melville died in 1906 at the age of eighty-four.

She's buried with her husband and three of their children in Wood-lawn Cemetery in the Bronx—
Her grave marker, nearly touching Melville's, is a cross adorned with climbing ivy.

In this blurry internet photo, the red container propped between their two gravestones is not, it turns out, a pint of beer but a canister of La Baleine coarse sea salt.

The brand with the spouting whale.

If my husband were here—he's somewhere near—I might show him the sea salt perched on the arm of Lizzie's cross.

And the hawk on the shed, and the buds of the bloodroot.

And the sticky notes on my desk, removed from due books, heaped in a neon pyre.

"We are poor passing facts," according to Robert Lowell and this blue sticky note.

Nevertheless, or consequently—
"It is pleasant," according to Elizabeth Hardwick, "to lay out the evidence."

I did, one morning, try, unsuccessfully, to discover how many copies of *Moby-Dick* exist in the world.

"Much remains unknown," writes one of Melville's biographers, "and always will."

I have reached, so many times, my free article limit.

But I found Marilynne Robinson's copy, filled with flags and "bent beyond repairing."

I found Susan Howe's heavily annotated copy, housed in the Beinecke Library at Yale.

And the copy in another Yale library that until 1930 was shelved under cetology.

I found Caleb Crain's old paperback copy, which still falls open to a homoerotic passage that disturbed and sustained him during his junior year in college, when he fell in love with a straight friend— "Lacking any idea what to do with my feelings, I sometimes stayed home alone in the evening, got drunk in a miserable way, and found a not-quite-comfort in reading and re-reading a passage from *Moby-Dick* that spoke to me strangely."

I found the copy that Darcey Steinke, hearing noises in the night, swung at the wall of her tent.

I found Stephen Colbert's copy, so rare and beautiful that he is reluctant to open it.

I found Melville's brother's copy, which was sold at auction in 2007 for $13,200, far below its estimated value.

And I found a "rain-spotted copy" purchased by Carl Van Doren in 1911 for twenty-five cents.

I found Melvillean Stanton Garner's Modern Library edition, which as a sailor in the Korean War he found in the library of a troopship, and which, given the crowded conditions of the bunk room, he read outdoors, on deck, in incessant rain—
"As I turned each soggy page, it came loose, and there was nothing else to do with the page other than throw it in the sea in a crumpled wet ball."

I found the copy an Englishwoman in 1870 gave to the captain of a trading schooner anchored off Samoa, telling him it was "the strangest, wildest, and saddest story" she had ever read, and which the captain read to the ship's crew from start to finish.

I found the "well-thumbed copy" belonging to Sir John Bland-Sutton, the doctor who, along with Henry A. Murray, performed an emergency appendectomy on the captain of the *Scythia* in 1924.

And the copy that Murray gave Freud in 1925—
Freud, Murray reported, found the whale symbolic.

I found @ericjohnkrebs's 1961 copy in which he found an old train ticket from the New York Central Railroad.

And @stefschwartz's lost copy which was found and turned in to the train station with her ticket still inside.

I found @ElizaCorlett's copy in which she found a £50 note, and @camhanlon777's copy in which he found $360 in twenties.

I found the copy that Alice Howland loses and then finds—in the microwave—in Lisa Genova's novel about a woman, age fifty, with early-onset Alzheimer's.

In William Gaddis's *The Recognitions* I found the copy that Mr. Feddle removes from his host's shelf and inscribes during a Christmas Eve party—
"He worked slowly and with care, unmindful of immediate traffic as though he were indeed sitting in that farmhouse in the Berkshires a century before."

I found Charles Olson's copy, a 1926 Modern Library edition which his parents gave to him for his nineteenth birthday, and in which his father, a postman, wrote the inscription, "When o'er this book, you cast your eyes, / Forget your studies and Mobylize."

I found the copy Melville inscribed to his father-in-law, and the one he inscribed to his brother-in-law—
dated January 6, 1853, though it was in fact 1854.

And the one he inscribed to his former shipmate, Henry F. Hubbard, whose annotation indicating that Pip was based on a real sailor named Backus was discovered in the early sixties by a friend of Hubbard's descendent—

"Think of all the years it had been there," she wrote to a book collector, "waiting for someone to find it."

I found the copy he gave to Hawthorne, which is unlocated and may never be found.

Perhaps some sleepless night I'll tell my husband about the three copies belonging to Rena Mosteirin, a poet and bookstore owner in New Hampshire.

There's the Norton Critical Edition she bought in college (edited by Harrison Hayford and the Biographer), its cover long gone.

There's the well-worn copy she found in a box on the street, then damaged further to make erasure poems.

And there's the 1956 Riverside Edition, its cover taped and retaped, which she opens daily—
"This may sound like a strange thing to say," she wrote in reply to my email, "but even though it destroys the book, I can tell that the book likes being opened each day."

Mosteirin, hoping to learn the novel's secrets, is tweeting *Moby-Dick*, one sentence per day—
She began ten years ago and is not yet halfway through.

No, she wrote, she doesn't know how many years remain, and she doesn't want to.

The sentence today (this twentieth day of March, AD 2021) is from Chapter 54, "The Town Ho's Story"—
And then, without at all alluding to the shovel, he pointed to three lads as

the customary sweepers; who, not being billeted at the pumps, had done lit-
tle or nothing all day.

Mosteirin says she looks forward to typing one of Melville's sentences
each morning—
Some days she reads it to her husband over coffee.

Acknowledgments

We are extraordinarily grateful to our many collaborators, most especially Amelia Atlas and Matt Weiland.

Thanks also to Huneeya Siddiqui, Dave Cole, Laura Goldin, and everyone at Norton.

We're grateful for the warm communities of both the Sewanee Writers' Conference and the Sewanee School of Letters, where we shared portions of the novel in progress.

And we're grateful for the support and editorial guidance of Adam Ross and Eric Smith at the *Sewanee Review*, in which early chapters of *Dayswork* first appeared.

We'd like to thank the Ohio Arts Council for its support of our project, and of artistic collaboration.

A number of scholars and artists responded to our queries in generous and generative ways, including Hilary Morgan, Rena Mosteirin, Steven Olsen-Smith, Elizabeth Renker, and Thomas Travisano.

Our days' work made us keenly appreciative of the labor and service of scholars and editors. We relied on the efforts of too many to name, but we would like to acknowledge the achievements of Hershel Parker, the Biographer, whose prodigious research and writing about Melville we found invaluable.